VILLAGE OF
SCARLET TEARS

J. D. CHANEY

World Castle Publishing, LLC
Pensacola, Florida
Copyright © J. D. Chaney 2019
Paperback ISBN: 9781950890705
eBook ISBN: 9781950890712
First Edition World Castle Publishing, LLC, October 7, 2019
http://www.worldcastlepublishing.com

Licensing Notes

Cover: Karen Fuller
Editor: Maxine Bringenberg

Chapter One

Rains continued to pummel the corrugated roof of the old schoolhouse. The staccato rhythms of the droplets, teaming with rusted tin, produced stentorian noises, making the teacher's efforts at holding a lecture nearly impossible.

Each of the windows, either cracked or completely shattered, failed to insulate the tiniest of sounds. He halted the lesson mid-sentence, throwing his arms up in capitulation. For almost the entire three weeks David Sherry had been in Mexico the storms had not let up, unmercifully hounding him, his students, and the little village of Mancha Negra. "That's it, class," he yelled in Spanish, then checking his watch, signaled that school was out for the day. David actually ended fifteen minutes early, feeling little pressure to maintain a strict timetable.

This is Mexico, he mused, not some damned stateside classroom. Anyway, he'd covered more material with these young people today than he would have in three days back home.

After twelve years of teaching in the seedy, industrialized waterfront area of southwest San Diego, David had had it. For years he'd waged a personal vendetta against the temptations of the street. But he knew his constant pep talks to his classes on the American dream were no match for the realities of poverty and despair that hung over the community in which he taught.

Now here he was, starting anew, peering over his lectern in unabashed glee at these young faces as they prepared for dismissal. The American's class was small: a total of thirteen students, and each as hungry to learn as the next. They seemed to lean on his every word, a perpetual look of concentration etched on their faces. With their dismissal, ten boys and three girls closed their tattered books and placed them inside their desks with an almost sacrosanct reverence.

"*Adios, Profesor,*" David heard them say in near unison as they spilled out the door and into the afternoon deluge. He watched from one of the windows as the young teens scurried down the mud laden road toward their village.

Mancha Negra was a speck of a town, forty miles south of the resort city of Acapulco, and anchored on the right fork of the Azoyu River. Its largely unpaved streets, lined with lush palms, bordered the whitewashed adobe homes of four hundred Mexican inhabitants whose livelihood was derived mainly from the sea. It seemed to be a tired village, with people seemingly moving inordinately slowly but accomplishing what needed to be done.

Regardless of the village's backwater appearance, the

Mexican government under the Salinas regime had begun instituting new laws regarding the bilingual education of its people, specifically those languages currently dominating international commerce.

And that's where David J. Sherry, B.A., M.A. English, entered the picture.

Returning to his desk, David leaned back in his chair and clasped his hands behind his head. He listened once more to the patterned strumming of the rain and allowed his mind to wander, recalling the circumstances that had led him to this enchanted hamlet.

The pressures of teaching at Albert Swann High had been enormous, and had taken a toll on most of the staff. For a dozen years, David endured daily confrontations with fractious students and incompetent administrators. But at some point late in his tenure, the popular teacher began succumbing to those pressures, finding succor in the proverbial bottle and losing a wife in the process. The ironic thing, however, was that no matter how chaotic his personal life became, he'd always maintained a high standard of teaching, arriving to work sober, clean shaven, and thoroughly prepared.

David demanded the most from himself and his students. Despite the dismal future that awaited the majority of his kids, it was his job to equip them for the real world. *And who knows*, he'd think to himself. *Perhaps one or two of them will get lucky and actually get out of this shit hole.*

David began his twelfth year at Swann with the

realization that it would be his last. Despite the obstacles David had done all he could, but now faced the realization that his head was no longer in the game. Education in the urban areas of California was changing, directing itself away from academics, and fostering instead the self-esteem aspects of the student. To a purist like David, this was the final blow. "Who do I look like, for Christ's sake?" he'd been heard to say to any staff member within earshot. "Some best-selling 'I'm okay, you're okay' guru? Is it going to be incumbent upon us teachers to instruct these kids on how to feel good about standing in an unemployment line? My God, what tripe."

The year passed by quickly. David taught as he always had, defying his superiors and worrying little about what they could do to him at this juncture. Besides, he'd already begun to seek greener pastures, cleaning up his own act, and putting into motion a number of inquiries regarding a place he'd been thinking about for a long time. It was common knowledge to most educators living near the border that Mexico was posting enlistment ads for teachers in U.S. papers in California and parts of the Southwest. Although many a complaining teacher from Swann threatened to take the plunge, only David applied.

Response from the neighboring country was immediate and favorable, prompting him to request — and receive — a leave of absence from his district. On his final day at work, Mr. Sherry bid adieu to his colleagues, grabbed his briefcase, and walked gamely through the graffiti-filled halls for what he hoped would be the last time. He bid goodbye to several of the teachers, all of whom had wished him luck. A look of envy from the older teachers reminded him that he was doing the right thing.

By the first week of August David was ready to go, his bags packed and stowed in the foyer of his vacated apartment. He decided to call his mother before heading for the airport, but hung up after the first ring, opting to avoid another lecture on the abandonment of job security. For now, a postcard from Mexico would have to do.

Arriving in Acapulco in the early afternoon, David caught a connecting flight to Tiapa where his interview, which he understood to be a mere formality, was held. Within less than an hour after his arrival, a contract containing a rather laughable salary was offered and duly signed. There had been little said of his assignment. All David knew for sure was that he'd been offered a position to teach an accelerated English class to a group of high school students in some small coastal village south of Tiapa. Frankly, that's the way he wanted it, finding joyful excitation in going pell-mell into what, for him, would be uncharted waters.

As they concluded negotiations, David was asked to wait in the lobby while someone rounded up a driver to take him to Mancha Negra. He shook hands with his interviewers and left the room, taking a seat near his luggage and fighting the ravages of a long, grueling day. All David wanted at this point was to get to the little pueblo, find himself a decent bed, and sleep undisturbed for as long as he could.

For a Yankee, David was more familiar with Mexico than most gringos. He had grown up in a Hispanic neighborhood in San Jose, California, picking up the language as a child. Years later, he spent his college summers trekking the land to the south, immersed in its diverse beauty and insouciant pleasures.

A small, round-faced man with horn rimmed glasses peeked his head through the entrance door of the lobby. "Señor Sherry?" he inquired. "I am Roberto Lopez, your driver." He quickly scampered to where the American had placed his bags and hefted one under each arm. "Now if you'll just follow me, please."

The brisk walk from the air-conditioned building to the Jeep found David bathed in sweat, his feet and hands beginning to swell from the blast furnace heat and heavy humidity. Even the slight trickling of rain that mysteriously appeared amid clear skies offered little aid.

Leaving Tiapa, the men motored along the highway before turning off on a narrow gravel road overrun by tufts of rich vegetation protruding through the blacktop surface. Six miles later they turned east along the Azoyu River onto a nearly impassable road, laden with deep ruts and jutting rocks. An agonizing two hours later they arrived at their destination. Lopez slowed the vehicle as they neared the village.

Mancha Negra appeared deserted. There were no children playing in the streets, no elderly women shuffling about their homes. The only moving object the men saw was a mangy, three-legged dog urinating precariously on a stack of adobe bricks.

"Where is everybody, Señor Lopez?" asked David.

Lopez smiled, revealing discolored, tobacco-stained teeth. "It is sundown, and the fishing boats are due in. Most of the people are down at *la boca* helping to clear the nets."

The two continued on, driving over the coarse, cobblestone main street. Midway through the village the angular teacher caught a glimpse of the plaza, a rectangle of sun-dried grass and crushed rock pathways which veered toward an old, wooden gazebo. Inside the airy structure sat a crudely sculpted statue of the virgin; at her feet lay two dolphins, eyeing her adoringly.

A sharp right-hand turn left them ascending a small rise where only the stubby trunks of recently cut pine trees remained. Upon reaching the top, the Mexican pointed to a rather unusual building situated just at the edge of the jungle. David did a double take and stared quizzically at the Disneyesque edifice. *This design is more appropriate for the Tyrolean Alps than Mexico*, he thought. The roof was steeply pitched. Long overhangs extended to the second floor of the house. Between the levels was a carved, stylized white lattice which separated the two levels and contrasted with the dark rosewood base. Brightly decorated shutters surrounded the front and back of the house. Directly over the entrance an extraordinarily large pair of elk antlers hung.

"This is it, Señor Sherry," said Lopez. "I thought you might want to see where you'll be staying before we take a look at your school."

Actually, he was hoping their first stop would be a cantina where he'd allow his parched throat a singular beer, but kept his mouth shut and nodded weakly. Approaching his quarters, David's eyes widened, utterly awestruck at what he was seeing. His driver seemed to sense his confusion and explained.

"It belonged to a German artist who had it built to remind him of home. He lived here, alone, for about four or five years. The reason I know this is because my brother helped build this house." Lopez reached for his breast pocket, pulling out a cigarette. "If you ask me, it's a house not many people of your profession could afford, under ordinary circumstances."

"Yes indeed," added David. "Whatever happened to the guy?"

"Señor Kaufman? Oh, he committed suicide," replied Lopez calmly. He continued, releasing a circular puff of grey smoke. "It appears he wasn't allowed to return to Germany for some reason. But the villagers in Mancha Negra think he lived too isolated a life up here, hardly ever coming off this knoll except for food and other supplies. All he seemed to do was paint."

Finding the tale disturbing, David fought off an involuntary shake but couldn't suppress his dismayed look.

"Don't worry, Señor Sherry," said the amused Mexican. "You'll find no ghosts in this house. Kaufman was kind enough to have shot himself down at the river's edge. When the police came to investigate they found no note, only several of his paintings ripped to shreds and thrown in the fireplace."

The men entered the house, its dark interior shadowing the sparse furniture. A large cardboard box filled with eating utensils and a half dozen neatly stacked pots and pans sat on the kitchen table. As they walked about the house, Lopez explained that immediately after the artist's death the police had sealed the home. Months later, after no heir came forth, the state of Guerrero's *Departmento de Educacíon* converted it to a teacher's residence.

After a cursory inspection of the house, Lopez suggested they drive to the school where David would be teaching. He agreed, following the bespectacled man out the door and toward the Jeep. As they worked their way back into town, Lopez steered in the direction of the plaza. Just beyond stood the church of San Cristóbal, with its brick exterior and severely handsome façade. On both sides of the church stood twin bell towers, separate structures anchored a few feet from the outer walls.

Lopez slowed as they passed the place of worship and came upon a corn field bisected by a dirt road. He put the Jeep into low and coaxed it along the furrowed course for about fifty yards before stopping at a clearing.

Dead ahead was the school, a building no larger than a two-car garage, with its metallic roof and red stucco walls. Leaving the Jeep, they walked around the weeded grounds until they came to the front doorstep. A large bronze placard embedded in the front door read, *Guerrero*

State School of Business and Language.

David chuckled to himself, thinking back to only a few hours ago when he first heard the school's name. He had envisioned some sort of ultra-modern, high-tech facility enveloped in glass and gaudily-angled architecture. Yet he was pleased with what he saw, thankful for the opportunity to get back to more simplified surroundings.

Opening the door, David entered first, nearly knocking over the lectern that had been leaning against a front row desk. He precariously squeezed by and reached for the light switch. Directly facing him were the student's desks, five neatly rowed tables with attached compartments, three deep and equally spaced. Happily for David, all fifteen pieces appeared to be relatively new. His desk, however, was another matter. He wondered from what second-rate pawn shop it had been confiscated.

At the far end of the room was a three-tiered bookshelf with two stacks of faded, lime green texts taking up the bottom two levels. David recognized them immediately as *Callam's Concise English Handbook*, textbooks so old and outdated that he remembered using them as a student himself. If memory served, they were quite unimaginative, albeit practical, books. A quick flip-through of one of them revealed the occasional missing page.

"Those are for you and your students," Lopez beamed. "I hope you'll find them useful."

"They'll do fine," David lied. He continued walking around the room, aware that the Mexican's eyes were following his own. When the teacher gazed at the condition of the windows, Lopez spoke up defensively.

"We will have someone out next week to install the windows. And if you happen to see anything else in need of repair, just make a list and I'll see that it gets done before school begins."

"Thanks. I appreciate it," said David. "By the way, you seem to be pretty familiar with things around here for just being a driver."

Lopez dropped his eyes in modesty. "No, senõr, I'm not only a driver, but also the head of maintenance for this district."

The explanation left the amused David smiling. "Roberto, I guess you're what we call a Jack of all trades."

They spent another ten minutes inventorying the room before David suggested they call it a day.

Full-scale rains accosted the two as they left the school, forcing them to scramble to the Jeep. The downpour had heavily weighted the tan canvas top that was stowed in the back, so they decided to forego it, buckling themselves in and speeding away in the open vehicle. Although thoroughly soaked by the time they managed to reach David's new home, neither man seemed particularly fazed. Their faces registered expressions belying the elements: for the Mexican, the look of one whose task had been completed, and for the American, one whose task was about to begin.

CHAPTER TWO

David stirred sluggishly, running a hand over bleary eyes. He listened as the approaching wind, which raced across a darkened sky, siphoned its way through a tiny orifice of shattered pane. Before he could react, the front door slammed shut, blowing a stack of uncorrected papers from his desk. He watched helplessly as they gravitated lazily away from the still unrepaired windows. Reluctantly, David rose from his seat and gathered them up before deciding he'd done enough work for the day.

The nearly mile-long walk to his new quarters felt good despite the rain. David had begun establishing a routine: he'd leave school in the afternoon and detour toward the *mercado* in search of fresh fruits and vegetables. From there he'd cross the street to the *panadaria* to purchase an occasional sugared roll or loaf of freshly baked bread. Little by little the villagers began acknowledging his presence, greeting David with slight nods or extending to him a polite, somewhat reserved, "*Hola, profesór.*" Eager to reciprocate, he'd slow his gait, hoping that maybe someone would engage him in a little conversation. But, as always, they'd pass by, leaving the American feeling like the town leper.

Although David hated to admit it, the feeling of abject loneliness began worming its way into his thoughts, something he hadn't counted on. The remedy was obvious. What he needed was a little company, particularly of the female variety. *After all*, David reflected, *I've been working my ass off since I first got here.*

The curriculum he'd developed was going well, and his students seemed to have taken to him and his teaching style. By the end of his first week of teaching, David had abandoned the usual disciplinary format, finding it unnecessary. He still insisted on a rigidly structured program, but made sure it also included a daily quota of laughter. It felt good to loosen the reins a bit. There was no denying that classroom productivity abounded, as did his emerging reputation. Professionally, all was right with the world. Now all he had to do was work on improving his social calendar.

Early morning brought with it a renewed expanse of blue sky, which tore through shreds of striated clouds. David shuffled from his living room into his kitchen, where he stood facing a sun-drenched window, his body still awakening from nine hours of deep slumber. He felt little need to hurry, opting to languish amid the slow-moving machinations of an early Saturday morning.

Today was going to be a special treat, David decided. The time had come when he felt he needed twenty-four hours of complete and utter irresponsibility and self-

15

indulgence. He had it all worked out. First thing on David's list was the beach: he'd do a little swimming, work on his tan, and sate himself on a Stuart Woods novel. Later in the day he'd return home, nap, clean up, and prepare for a night on the town, such as it was. Upon his first day of arriving at Mancha Negra, David had noticed a small cantina at the far end of town. Tonight he'd pay it a visit.

An extra cup of coffee jolted him into action. By nine o'clock he'd begun walking to the beach, his backpack toting a sandwich, towel, book, and number fifteen sunscreen. David passed two fishermen repairing their nets near the mouth of the estuary and smiled. The fishermen's creased faces passively returned his glance before resuming their activities.

"To hell with them," he said aloud. "Nothing's going to ruin this day."

David sat on his towel, his knees pulled into his chest. He hadn't read; he hadn't swum; in fact, he hadn't done much of anything in the hour he'd been there but walk idly along the shallows, kicking at the warm, aqua waters, whose glistening foam engulfed his feet. For as long as he could remember, the mesmeric power and splendor of the sea had a way of filling him with an innate peace that he could always rely on, no matter how much turmoil existed in his life. Turning into the wind, David felt the sudden urge of wanting to fly. Arms cast out to his side, the teacher smiled inwardly, amused by his puerile behavior and overwhelmed by a sudden reaffirmation of who he was and why he'd come to Mancha Negra.

As he reached his towel, David picked up the book laying near his feet, and was about to read when he caught sight of the two men he'd seen earlier. They were struggling to get their battered skiff past the break waters. After hurdling the first couple of waves they worked furiously at hoisting the tiny sail, expertly maneuvering it to capture the pockets of wind that would eventually blast them into the calm sea. David watched in fascination, completely absorbed with the struggle. Again he discarded his novel, choosing to study their progress well into the afternoon.

David returned home late and napped soundly, dazed by hours spent in the sun. He woke at seven o'clock that evening, ate quickly, and showered, drying himself in front of the bathroom mirror. The day's session in the sun had tanned his face and body a deep copper, accentuating his green eyes and flashing white teeth. Moving closer to the mirror, he sought a more critical accounting of his body. For a forty-one-year-old man, he had still maintained his rugged good looks. His athletic body remained muscular yet lean, and sat well on his six-foot frame. The hair had grayed somewhat, but at least, thank God, it was still there.

David moved to the bedroom and dressed in a starched blue button down shirt, khaki pants, and sockless brown loafers. He doused himself with a splash of French cologne, an ancient birthday present from his ex-wife, and checked himself one last time in the mirror. A final glance at his watch indicated 8:10 p.m.

Anxiously, David looked about the house, making sure it wasn't too cluttered. "You never know," he conceded." I might get lucky." He popped a stick of gum in his mouth and exited.

The leisurely walk to the cantina took twenty minutes. Careful not to mess up his freshly polished shoes, David took advantage of a full moon, which guided him away from the road's water-filled divots. As he approached the village's outskirts he noticed that the streets grew quiet, except for a handful of *camposinos* amicably loitering outside the entrance of the cantina.

Drawing nearer, David recognized a mint-condition 1963 Chrysler Imperial parked in front of the cantina. Curious, he strolled by the automobile, marveling at its glossy blue exterior and white-wall rayon tires. David's eyes moved upward to the classically stacked horizontal grill supporting a stylized gold embossed emblem containing the initials T.A. He rounded the car, hopping up onto the sidewalk, and walked cautiously past the assembled group of men into the Club El Gato.

The room was sparsely lit, with low wattage overhanging bulbs painting the walls in elongated silhouettes. There were twelve tables in all, including a horseshoe-shaped bar that accompanied eight stools. At one end of the bar, a fifties-type juke box vibrated to the strains of blaring Mexican standards. The smells of stale tobacco and perspiration were intense.

Idle talk and boisterous bantering, which moments ago had been free flowing, came to an abrupt halt. Disquieting murmurs and accusatory undertones snaked their way through the room, while several pairs of eyes riveted themselves on the intruder.

David stepped tentatively up to the bar, catching the attention of the bartender. "*Cervesa, por favór,*" he requested. As he reached for his wallet, David felt dabs of moisture encircling the folds of his newly pressed shirt. He paid for his beer and, with his bottle in hand, turned in the direction of the dance floor. He was intent on enjoying himself, no matter what.

David downed the beer quickly, hoping it would steady his nerves, and immediately ordered a second. This one he intended to nurse, realizing the need to control his drinking. As the bartender handed him the brew, David heard someone directly behind him shout, "Pepe, please, put the Americano's beer on my tab."

The stunned teacher torqued his neck in search of the voice. There, positioned at a corner table near the entrance, sat an immensely heavy man in his early sixties. He appeared nattily attired in a cream colored silk suit and ruffled pink shirt, which he left half opened, exposing a handful of grey, curled chest hairs. On his lap David noticed a neatly creased Panama hat, which the man had been using to fan himself.

At his table sat two women, one dark haired, the other a bleach blonde. Each was heavily made up and seductively dressed, making it difficult for David to decipher their ages.

"Please señor, join us," bellowed the rotund man in passable English. He extended an open hand in the direction of an empty chair. Welcoming any kind of

19

company for the moment, David gave an indifferent shrug of his shoulders, grabbed his beer, and ambled over to the table.

"Thanks for the beer. I'm —"

"Señor David Sherry," interrupted the Mexican. "This introduction is long overdue. Actually, I've wanted to meet you for quite some time. My name is Tito Alvarez."

David's eyes widened. "How did you know my name?"

Tito adjusted his voice, reverting to his native tongue. "It's my job to know all the good citizens of Mancha Negra. You, of course, are the American teacher who has come to educate some of our outstanding youths. A very noble deed, if I may say so."

"I welcome the opportunity," remarked David, his eyes returning to normal. He took a small sip of his drink and stared again at the dance floor, happy to see the revival of activities among the customers. Feeling more relaxed, David permitted himself a look at the two girls flanking Tito. Both appeared bored and disinterested in the evening's festivities. The blonde was rigorously examining her fingernails, spreading each digit in search of the proper sheen. The other woman had removed a small compact from her purse and was copiously applying a purplish lipstick to an already abundantly lacquered pair of lips.

"May I introduce my companions to you, Señor Sherry?" Putting his meaty arm around the long nailed girl, he declared, "This is Gloria. Very pretty, don't you think?" David agreed, nodding politely to the woman who smiled coquettishly in return: a look well-rehearsed and geared for men like himself.

"And this one here is Margarita. She may appear bashful, but I assure you, she is a tornado." Tito beckoned her forward into the light, all the while staring at her with a lascivious grin. Margarita smiled as well, and in jetting her face into the lighting, revealed an acne filled forehead, poorly hidden by gobs of Max Factor's finest. Jesus, David reasoned, *I'll bet this one isn't more than seventeen.*

Returning his attention to Tito, David asked hesitantly, "Uh, may I ask, señor, what you do for a living?"

The Mexican laughed deeply, throwing his head back and exposing multiple sets of chins. "I am a provider of sorts. A lesser man might call me a pimp, but those who know me will tell you I offer invaluable services to our community."

Unaccustomed to such directness, David tittered nervously and reached again for his beer. But the perceptive pimp intercepted him, lightly grasping his wrist. "Señor Sherry, if I've embarrassed you, I am sorry. I only wanted you to know that I provide a happy service. My girls are clean and well paid, and they're free to refuse anyone's offer no matter what their status." Having given his lecture, Tito sat back, awaiting David's reaction.

A wave of uneasiness swept over the teacher. Regretting for a moment that he ever came into the cantina, he scanned the room again in anticipation of stares that proved to be nonexistent. Tito removed his hand from

David's wrist, allowing the younger man to pursue his drink. David took a long draft, feeling the speedy effects of the alcohol bolstering his confidence. "Look, Señor Alvarez, I only came in here to have a drink and maybe a little...fun."

"You want fun?" asked Tito. "Then fun is what you'll get." He grabbed an arm from each girl and pulled them closer to the table, closer to David. The whores leaned forward. Their loose-fitting low-cut blouses allowed him to cast his eyes on their alluring breasts, so tanned and full. He squirmed in his chair and felt a distinct warmth rising from his loins. David had been far too long without a woman, but an odd sense of caution kept him at bay.

Before David could decline Tito's offer, the dark haired woman spoke. "Come, dance with me," she purred, pulling David from the chair and directing him to the dance floor.

Amid several other couples they began to dance, tentatively at first, until Margarita drew into him, pressing herself against his chest. Her inguinal movements aroused him, easing his earlier trepidations. David's body tingled as she slipped an arm around his waist, moving her fingers along his spine until they reached his neck.

He heard himself moan as she massaged the nape of his neck with thumb and forefinger before turning his face to meet hers. Expertly the young whore parted her lips, beckoning him to her with a glint of tongue. David responded and kissed her hard and long, evoking a pleasantly surprised hum from Margarita.

Despite the lightheadedness he was feeling, David continued his embrace, consumed and intoxicated by her vaporous heaving. A muted drumming slowly began traversing his spine, accentuating his senses. He marveled at the coolness of the pulsations, which seemed to prolong and yet ration the impulses of his stoking passions. Fearing that the effects of Margarita's embrace would soon wane, David struggled to remain entranced in this prickling rapture.

But something already seemed different. The bestial pleasures began mutating, bursting into hot, penetrating stabs which centered in the small of his back. David's body stiffened, his balance seemingly impaired. He turned loose of Margarita, and caught from the corner of his eye the flashing remnants of an elbow removing itself from his back. David tumbled to the floor, where he was inadvertently fallen upon by one of the other dancing couples. Looking up in disbelief, he watched as a forest of legs scrambled about the room. Helplessly he searched for Margarita, only to discover she'd disappeared among the confusion.

"I'll kill you," came a baritoned voice, somewhere to David's left. "You are my woman," the man continued, his words slurred with drink.

"I am nobody's woman," came a shaky rejoinder. "I'm warning you, Vega. Leave me the hell alone."

David flinched, realizing that the object of the man's scorn was standing only a few feet away from him: a diminutive looking girl in spiked heels, and her even smaller, bushy haired dancing partner, who was attempting to maneuver himself behind her.

David got to his feet, unaware that the other patrons had fled from the dance floor, leaving only the accuser, the dancing couple, and himself, who happened to be positioned between them. Too frightened to move, he stood motionless as the drunk approached clumsily, a pearl-handled dagger in his right hand.

The man was a few inches shorter than David, but more powerfully built, his T-shirt straining to contain his massive neck and chest. As he neared the American, this man called Vega smiled sardonically, tapping the blade to the back of his hand. "Perhaps you would like a little taste of this too, huh, gringo?"

His eyes glued to the knifed hand, David said nothing. Then, looking up for only an instant, he winced, catching sight of the attacker. A lone brown eye returned his gaze, while the other, a clouded, lifeless orb, lay tucked in its socket. David could smell his ranking breath, but knew better than to turn away. Vega's smile had dissolved into a scowl.

As the drunk brushed by, David exhaled silently, chillingly aware of the man's deliberately hostile movements, which only moments ago had appeared awkward and erratic. With a minimum of motion David rotated his shoulders, and viewed Vega as he moved in the direction of the young woman.

Inexplicably, David broke toward the man's back, diving at his ankles. But Vega, warned by the approaching footsteps, managed to repel his rival's lunge, catching David between the eyes with the heel of his boot before dropping to one knee. Vega fought to recapture his balance, then turned to face the prostrate American. To David's chagrin, his opponent still held the knife. With no other options to pursue, David forced himself to his feet and continued his reluctant battle with the stronger Vega.

An ill-timed thrust from Vega's knife prompted David to skirt to his right. Realizing Vega had left himself momentarily open, David recoiled and surged ahead, hurling himself on the Mexican's chest and knocking him to the floor. Vega lay still, gasping loudly for air. David managed to pry open Vega's fist, but as he grabbed the knife Vega lifted a knee, striking the stunned American squarely in the groin and leaving him floundering helplessly atop his assailant.

David groaned flatly and felt a near loss of consciousness. His adrenalin, almost depleted, could do little to rekindle whatever recuperative powers remained. He could sense the body beneath him regenerating power at a pace quicker than his own. The realities of escaping this man's grasp would be difficult, but he had no choice. In an excruciating move, David pushed forward, straddling the man's waist. With the Mexican's good eye still appearing void, David hoped that perhaps he might be able to clear himself of the immobile figure.

But as he began to rise, Vega suddenly pitched forward, catching the American with the knife and carving an eight-inch gash from his elbow to his wrist. A second thrust attempt by Vega struck underneath David's flexed knee and into an overturned chair. With the blade solidly embedded in one of the chair's legs, the two men scrambled for the handle. David reached first, but a giant paw — even larger than Vega's — topped his, squeezing his fingers together so tightly they resembled a unit no thicker than his thumb.

"Enough. Maximilian," ordered Tito.

Upon command, the pimp's giant bodyguard consented, releasing his grip on David and helping him to his feet. Maximilian then offered a hand to Vega, who waved him off bitterly and pushed himself to one knee. The wild-eyed attacker watched suspiciously while Tito removed himself from his chair and approached David. The pimp produced a kerchief, which he used to bind David's wounds.

"Pepe, find Teresa, quickly."

"Si, Señor Alvarez," countered the goateed man behind the bar. He quickly shed his apron and dashed for the door.

Tito smiled warmly at David. "Do not worry, señor. It does not look too bad." David wanted to respond, but weakened by the loss of blood, mouthed an incoherent remark. The kick he'd endured earlier left him feeling top heavy, and he could feel himself teetering to one side. Tito signaled for the six-foot nine-inch Maximilian to escort David to a nearby table, and then turned his attention to Vega. The pimp closed to within inches of the man's face.

"I know you," he simmered. "Or, I know about you.

26

Vega, isn't it? Isn't that what Lucy called you?" The assailant said nothing, his weight shifting from one leg to another, his stance open and defensive. "You're not from this village, but I remember seeing you here once before. Several months ago one of my girls was attacked in her room. Fortunately, her screams brought Maximilian to her rescue, but not before she'd been beaten and had her face carved up. Her attacker somehow managed to escape, which was a real pity. The poor child was hysterical, mouthing nonsense at the top of her lungs. At least we thought it was nonsense. She kept repeating that her assailant possessed the eye of the devil." Moving even closer, Tito peered deliberately into Vega's lifeless eye. "I believe, señor, that you are that devil."

Vega broke the stare, his good eye fidgeting from left to right. The pimp was now backed by two additional men, each well-conditioned and primed for action. Vega's brain raced for a compromising solution, while his instincts sought more dangerous options.

Feigning a lunge at Tito, Vega broke toward the fallen chair, where he grabbed for the embedded knife. The angle of his grip promptly snapped the blade in half, forcing him to rise with less than half of the nine-inch blade in his hand. Twice he slashed the air with it in a semi-circlular motion, forcing Tito's men to slow their forward movements. When he felt enough distance between himself and Tito and his men, Vega quickly reversed his field and sprang in the direction of the back door.

An aging, grey haired *camposino*, who'd been sitting

unseen near the darkened exit, rose in protest, startling the fleeing man. Vega instinctively hammered a thunderous fist into the man's midsection. As the old man began to fall, Vega caught him, lifted him off the ground, and hurled him into the advancing men.

The *camposino's* body hit the man closest to Vega, knocking him down and taking Tito's other man with him. Amid the calamity, Vega sprung for the exit and escaped into the night.

CHAPTER THREE

David woke with a start, his mouth dry and his vision blurred and distorted. He strained to regain his sensibilities, crying out in frustration. As he lurched forward from the bed, a searing charge of electric pain originating from his heavily bandaged wound struck his innards, evoking immediate retching.

A moment later a trapezoid of light splayed through the pitch of the room, followed by the sounds of shuffling feet. David reared back, hitting his head on a warm, dank pillow.

"Welcome back, Señor Sherry. You've had quite a sleep." The voice was soft and assuring.

Taking a small towel from a nearby dresser, the owner of the voice hovered over him and wiped away the dried spittle from his mouth and chin.

"My name is Teresa. I am the one who fixed your arm." David's swollen eyes opened, but remained unfocused. He knew her face was slender, her hair dark. When she passed a weightless hand in front of him, he detected the scent of lilac.

Clenching his teeth, David asked, "Where am I?"

"In my house," came the voice. "You lost a lot of blood, so we had to move you here."

"Are you a doctor?"

Teresa laughed. "I wish that were true, but no. I am a nurse...well, sort of. I attended nursing school for a while...." Her voice trailed off. Although unable to see, David sensed a touch of melancholy in her words. "Now you must rest. You lost a lot of blood. I will look in on you later." She bent over him and pulled a sheet to his chest. Uncertain of the exact position of her face, David removed a hand from under the sheet, offering it to her.

"Thank you, Teresa," he said, feeling her soft palm slipping into his. "I'm very grateful."

"It was nothing, a very routine stitch job." She guided her other hand to David's forehead, estimating his temperature. "Enough talk for now. Get some sleep, and if you're strong enough tomorrow we'll bathe you. You're starting to stink." Teresa gave him a quick smile, unaware of his impaired sight, and left. She shut the door and sealed off any remaining vestiges of light. The dark seemed to enhance David's exhaustion, and although alone, he no longer felt frightened. He closed his eyes and fell into a deep sleep.

David awoke the following morning to the sounds of distant murmurs. He tested his eyes and found them vastly improved. Colors and shapes came into view, bringing a toothy grin to his face. The pain in his arm hadn't diminished, but his head felt clear and devoid of any discomfort. A growling stomach reminded him it needed attention as well.

Tito Alvarez was standing at the foot of the bed, his eyebrows furrowed in a look of concern. "Señor Sherry," he whispered. "How are you feeling?"

David opened his mouth to respond when Teresa approached from another room.

"Please, Tito, not now. Let me feed and clean him up first."

Tito looked at David and raised his hands in submission. "All right, all right, Teresa. He's yours for now, but I'll be back in one hour." As he exited, David noticed Maxmilian falling in beside Tito and accompanying him outside.

Teresa's face was half hidden under a mound of clean bedding she carried, but as she drew closer he saw her clearly for the first time. David's breathing quickened. Never had he seen anyone so beautiful. Tall and willowy, the ebony-haired woman glided across the room, the subtle contours of her hips accentuated in a white, translucent cotton dress. A flawlessly skinned profile revealed a finely sculpted, aquiline nose, whose nostrils flared over a full and sultry mouth. He placed her age at twenty-five, but her demeanor was that of a much older woman.

After setting the bedding on top of the dresser, Teresa walked to the nightstand, poured a glass of water from a ceramic pitcher, and offered it to David. He managed to prop himself up and eagerly accepted the water, downing it greedily.

"Very good, señor. Your color is returning, and so is

your strength, I see. I think by this evening you can go home."

David grunted and asked for more water, which he drank with equal gusto. After a moment he lay back, feeling much better, but filled with new concerns.

"Teresa, my class, my students. I—"

"Don't worry," interrupted the woman. "Tito contacted Señor Lopez, who has arranged for someone to take your class while you recuperate. You'll be back teaching in a couple of days."

Shaking his head in disbelief, David produced a sly smile. "Good old Lopez, the Jack of all trades."

"What was that?"

"Oh nothing, just thinking out loud." David released a long breath, greatly relieved that his job was not in jeopardy.

Accepting the empty glass from David, Teresa marched to the other side of the bed.

"Now, as I said last night, you smell. So, we're going to give you a bath. Gloria," she called out. "I need you now." Another woman entered and David recognized her as one of the young prostitutes from the cantina.

Gloria vanished into an adjoining room and David heard the faint sounds of bath water being drawn. Nervously, he looked under the sheets and realized for the first time he was completely naked. It also occurred to David that during the entire time he'd been there, he had no recollection of relieving himself. *God*, he thought, disturbed. *Did Teresa take care of that too?*

The two women moved toward him from the left side of the bed, and gently eased David to an upward position. They swung their arms under his frame and walked the naked teacher toward the bath.

"Oh señor, you are a big one," snickered the younger woman. Teresa laughed as well, leaving David wondering what exactly they were referring to.

The bath made him feel much better, and as he returned to his bed, another woman—this one unknown to David—carried in a tray of soup and warm tortillas. She fed him in silence while Teresa and Gloria scurried about, tidying up the room.

"Ah, you are awake." The recognizable voice of Tito Alvarez startled David. Tito entered the room alone, and signaled for the women to leave them.

"Ten minutes, Tito—no more," warned Teresa, shaking her finger at him as she and the other women filed out of the room.

David's slack hand greeted Tito. "Señor Alvarez, I'd like to thank you for all you've done. If it hadn't been for you and Teresa, I shudder to think where I'd be right now."

Tito delicately placed his great bulk on the edge of the bed. "It's not me you need to thank, but Teresa. All I did was protect our town's investment. Whether you realize it or not, you are a much needed commodity here in our little village. If we Mexicans are going to progress into the twenty-first century, we'll need dedicated people like you working with our young men and women. This is the only way we can survive.

"My dream is for Mancha Negra and the hundreds of villages like it to become self-sufficient and proud of their newfound intellect. We want our communities to be known as something more than quaint little tourist havens with agreeable weather and amusing customs. Look around you, Señor Sherry," he continued. "Mexico is a country with tremendous potential. For now we will rely on outside support, but someday…someday we hope to be considered equals of our friends to the north." Tito, suddenly aware that he'd been lecturing, laughed. "There I go again, speaking like some damned politician running for office."

David smiled in return. He liked this man, sensed sincerity in Tito's words, and wondered how he'd ended up a pimp. Someday he hoped to ask him, but for now David had a more important question.

"Señor Alvarez, I'd…ah…I'd like to know more about Teresa, the nurse. Can you tell me something about her?"

Tito sighed and dropped his eyes.

"Teresa Maria Santos is the kindest, most loving woman alive. She was born in your country — Albuquerque, to be exact — where her parents moved to in order to find work. They stayed there for six or seven years and then returned here, unable to make a decent living in the States. Teresa's parents and older brother were killed in a car accident about four years ago, outside of Mexico City. She'd been attending a private nursing school near the university, but was forced to return home after the tragedy for financial

34

reasons. What little money the family had went to Teresa's studies and living expenses. And, to make matters worse, she was left with her family's debts, as well as her father's overdue payments on his skiff."

David shook his head. "Is there no one else she can turn to?"

Tito paused at David's question, staring at his fingertips. "Yes señor, she has an uncle who has offered to help. But Teresa is a stubborn child. For several weeks after her return to Mancha Negra, she refused to accept any money from him. Finally they reached an agreement of sorts. She wouldn't take any handouts, but offered to work for him until she'd saved enough to pay off her parents' debts and return to nursing school."

"Who is this man?" queried David.

The answer came, but not from Tito. The door to the room opened and an unseen voice called out. "Are you still hounding the poor man?" The figure of Teresa emerged, her hands on her hips, a pronounced pout on her lips. "Really, Uncle, you're as talkative as an old woman."

Stunned disbelief registered on David's face. "You're Tito's niece?" he asked, his voice an octave higher than normal.

"Of course, señor. You did not know?" She moved to Tito and placed her arm into his, kissing him on the cheek. "This meddlesome old bachelor is all the family I have left since the accident, and although we have our differences, I love him dearly."

The pimp beamed at her words, thrusting a prideful

chest forward. He glanced at David, hoping to find him enamored by her comments as well, then cleared his throat for effect. "I'd better be going. I've several business matters that need taking care of. Señor Sherry, when you have recovered, I'd be honored to show you Mancha Negra, and perhaps give you an idea of why I'm so passionate about it. This is a village untouched by those of you in the north. We remain traditionally Mexicanos."

"Uh.... Oh, yes, I'd like that very much," David stammered. Tito left the room with little fanfare, leaving David and Teresa alone. An agonizing few seconds of silence prompted the uncomfortable American to initiate conversation. "He's quite a guy, your uncle."

"Yes he is. There isn't one person in this town whom he hasn't done something for."

"Um...do people mind that he is a...?"

"A pimp, Señor Sherry?" she finished. "Tito Alvarez is no ordinary pimp. He could be a very wealthy man with his stable of girls, yet he takes very little for himself. Why, last year two of the girls got married, and Tito provided them with a lavish wedding. Even Father Gomez, the local priest, holds him in high esteem. He has learned to compromise and forgive Tito's discretions because of his charitable deeds."

"I'm sorry, Teresa, I just thought—"

"That's just it, señor," Teresa continued in her admonishing voice, "You did not think. Who do you think bought your school all those new desks?" David blinked in surprise. "That's right, señor. Tito even made sure each student was properly presented to you in new clothes—which, again, he purchased."

David held her stare meekly, not sure how to react. It was incomprehensible to him how anyone could hold such allegiance to a man of this profession. But then again, he'd never known anyone of Tito Alvarez's caliber.

Sensing that her indignation had somewhat subsided, David pursued his line of questioning, anticipating the disturbing answer the young Mexicana was about to give.

"Teresa, can you tell me what it is you do for your uncle?"

"Certainly," she replied nonchalantly. "I'm one of his girls."

Only an Academy-Award winning actor would have been able to mask the disappointment David felt at that moment. Crestfallen, he fell back on his pillow, his face contorted with disgust. "But why, for God's sake? You're a bright, beautiful woman."

"No brighter or more beautiful than the others. Besides, it's not as if I'm going to be doing this for the rest of my life. Once I save enough money and pay off my family's debts, I will return to school."

"But I heard your uncle say he'd gladly give you the money, and that it wasn't necessary to…uh…do this line of work."

"Oh señor, but it is. Never will I accept charity, even from my uncle. As long as I'm capable of making a living, I will. Where else could I make the kind of money I'm now making? Tell me, please. A clerk perhaps? A waitress, a vendor? Really, Señor Sherry, I'd be an old woman before I'd saved up enough money to return to school.

"Besides, I feel good about what I do. I'm no trollop. You may not believe this, but I don't go to bed with many of the men who pay me. Some are lonely or elderly, and want only to talk or be held. Others are frightened young boys from the fields who are experiencing a woman for the first time. I use many of these situations to practice my true vocation on them. I nurse them through their tribulations, I listen empathetically, and offer advice when I can. I believe people who do this in your country are called sexual surrogates, are they not? Rarely do I fuck for money without extracting some sort of lesson from it."

David's eyes narrowed, scrutinizing the rationality of her words. He was clearly captivated by her freshness and unique perceptions of life. "How does your uncle feel about this?"

"He doesn't like it, and feels guilty for having accepted my deal. I've tried to have him look logically at what I do, but he still feels uncomfortable. Tito thinks it's okay for the other girls because they have little or no education, but for his niece, it's not acceptable."

"How much longer do you think it'll take you to save up the money to quit?"

"I figure another year and I'm through. I'm steadily paying off my debts, and soon I'll begin saving for my return to school. Room and board is not cheap in the city."

"Whew," said David, shaking his head. "This has been quite an education for me. I'll give you this, señorita, you certainly know what you want out of life, and sure as hell aren't afraid to use any means possible to achieve it."

She laughed easily. "I was raised to be frank and realistic. And what about you? Can you say the same about yourself?"

"Me?" David paused, considering her question. "Well, yes, I think so. If I weren't, I don't think I'd be here teaching right now."

"Good," Teresa replied. "Then you won't mind my next question." She walked over to the window and opened it a fraction. With her back to David, she asked, "Do you hate what I do?"

He needed time to think this one over, to choose his words carefully. As of that moment, David had ambivalent feelings about the tarnished Mexican beauty. He was genuinely captivated by her presence and compassion, yet repelled by her sexual indifference. The answer he gave surprised even him. "I don't know," he blurted. "I guess it's your life, and you're entitled to do with it what you will."

She turned from the window for a moment, her thinly veiled smile reduced to a neutral expression. "Somehow I'm having a hard time believing that, Senor Sherry."

David studied the stillness of her face, masked in the weariness of hidden insecurities, and wondered for the moment who was indeed the real patient.

"Okay," she said, breaking from her funk with a quick shake of her hair. "It's time for you to leave the nest. This evening after supper, I'll walk you back to your home. Do you feel strong enough?"

"Absolutely. I could do with a little fresh air."

He was also anxious to return to his home and his work, but glad to be once more in the company of Tito's young niece.

His dinner arrived in the evening, delivered not by Teresa but by an elderly woman who told him Teresa would return in an hour to take him home. Disappointed, he picked at his food, finished dressing himself, and waited for Teresa. David surprised himself at how constantly he thought of her. *Hold it, old boy,* he uttered to himself. *You're acting like a smitten teen. Don't let your loneliness, or for that matter, your horniness, get the better of you.*

He was just beginning to convince himself when in walked Teresa. She looked different, older, her hair curled and piled on top of her head. Her face was heavily made up, and she wore lipstick that matched the dark, form-fitting dress, cinched at the waist and plunging at the neckline.

"I'm sorry I'm late, Señor Sherry, but I had an engagement. Are you ready to go?"

David knew all too well what she meant, and struggled to control his irritation at her words. "Don't bother," he hissed. "I can make my own way home." Grabbing his jacket from behind a chair, David wobbled toward the door. But without warning, a slight queasiness germinated from his intestines and stopped him in his tracks. "My stomach," he said, his face suddenly pale. "I think—"

"You'll be all right," assured Teresa. "You've just eaten

your first solid foods in almost two days." No longer in the mood to protest, David accepted Teresa's arm. "Come, Señor Sherry, let's go home."

The leisurely walk up the road lessened much of David's ire, and together they gazed at the stars which were only now becoming visible in the twilight.

"I think you are anxious to return to work, no?" asked Teresa.

"You bet. I was becoming too spoiled being waited on hand and foot. Although, if it weren't for the fact that I'm really enjoying teaching this year, I might have tried to convince you that I needed more rehab time."

This drew a caustic laugh from Teresa. "Just what I thought. Another American attempting to take advantage of us poor Mexicanos."

The two continued their stroll up the hill, with Teresa intermittently offering a steady hand to her weakened patient. Both seemed consciously aware of their increasing attraction to one another. Just before reaching the house, David slipped his hand out of Teresa's and moved it delicately behind her shoulder. Teresa, for her part, did not resist, inching herself closer to him.

When the two approached the front door, David turned, facing Teresa. "Look, I really can't thank you enough—"

"Shhh," she whispered, drawing an index finger up to her lips. "We've already been through this. You're alive and well, and that's all that counts." Teresa tugged lightly on his neck, bringing him in position for a soft kiss on his cheek. "Now I must go. Try to keep those bandages clean for the next twenty-four hours." Before he had a chance to react, Teresa pivoted on her toes and bounded down the hill.

Stunned and breathless, David called out weakly, "When will I see you again?"

A faceless voice yelled back, "Soon, Señor Sherry. I promise."

David gleamed, delighted at her response. He continued to watch Teresa, entranced in the kinetics of her perky jaunt, when something suddenly occurred to him. Stepping forward, he cupped his hands around his mouth and yelled as loudly as he could, "One more thing. No more Señor Sherry, okay? It's David, just plain David."

CHAPTER FOUR

The American teacher returned to work and, for the next week, immersed himself in his vocation, the cathartic image of Teresa periodically interrupting his thoughts. By the following week the images grew stronger, and the need to see her became imperative.

David would find himself gravitating from his lectern to one of the windows, where he'd peer over the rows of corn that veered toward the village, hoping to discover the shapely presence of Teresa making her way to the school. *She promised she'd see me,* he thought. *Those were her words to me.*

On Saturday afternoon the rains reappeared, only this time with greater force. The main road to and from Mancha Negra was washed out. Sections of the village lost electrical power, and were forced to survive by candlelight and home fires. David's house, however, had been spared of any of nature's inconveniences. The teacher brooded, his listless frame centered on the couch. He stared glumly at the remaining embers of a once comfortable fire.

"Has she forgotten me already?" he heard himself

say. "Perhaps she just doesn't want to see me. God, what a pompous ass I've been. She's right. Who the hell am I to judge her?"

David sighed, sagging even deeper into the couch. There had to be a way to prove to her he wasn't the obtuse, judgmental idiot she'd experienced several days ago.

Forcing himself to his feet, David began pacing, incognizant of the earsplitting cracks of thunder that railed over the hills. His peregrinating footsteps, which looped from kitchen to living room, continued for nearly an hour before coming to an abrupt halt.

"Yes, dammit," he proclaimed loudly, his thinking suddenly clear.

David sprang for the door, grabbing his coat and ball cap, and dashed out into the damp twilight. Ignoring the rain, David moved to the shoulder of the road and sloshed through the briny rivulets of mud leading to the cantina. He wasn't quite sure what he intended to say to Teresa, other than how sorry he was. No lectures, no speeches, just a few honest minutes of her time. David hoped he'd find her alone, although he knew weekends were an active time for Tito's girls. Anyway, he resolved that if he had to, he'd buy her time just like any other customer.

He hurdled the steps leading to the cantina in one leap and, as he approached the door, heard the familiar sounds of the jukebox. Unrecognizable faces huddled near the entrance overhang in an attempt to stay dry. David nodded, and was pleasantly surprised to see them return the courtesy.

The Club El Gato was sparsely occupied with patrons due to the early hour, but the agitating haze of cigarette smoke hadn't lessened since his last visit. David spotted Teresa seated near her uncle. Drawing a deep breath and exhaling in tiny increments, he marched steadily toward them. The two seemed preoccupied, and did not notice him until he'd reached the table. Positioned between Tito and Teresa was a type of ledger, with names and figures listed in vertical columns.

"Hello Tito, Teresa," David began. "Am I interrupting?"

Both looked up simultaneously, Teresa appearing more surprised than her uncle.

"Señor David," acknowledged Tito. "How are you?" Tito pulled an empty chair from the table. "I'm glad to see you looking so well. Don't you agree, Teresa?"

Teresa closed the ledger and smiled uncomfortably. "Yes," she concurred. Despite David's hopes, she said nothing further, pushing herself away from the table. After adjusting a brightly colored shawl over her bare shoulders, Teresa stood up, facing the men. "I'm sorry, but you both must excuse me. I have an appointment." She turned away so as not to see David's face.

Whatever words David had been rehearsing to discuss with Teresa had completely vanished. Flustered, he watched as she sauntered to the bar, where a slender, fresh-faced youth with large sunken eyes awaited her. The boy appeared nervous, unable to meet her stare. He rubbed a sweaty hand across his shirt.

"Is that her appointment, Tito?" asked David, slinging

his head in the direction of the young man.

The pimp nodded silently, looking all the while at David's morose posture. Calmly he reached out and patted the American's arm. "Señor David, please remember this is only business to Teresa. She has no special interest in this boy."

"I don't care," declared David. "She shouldn't be doing this kind of thing at all." He rose from his chair, hitting the table with his thigh and knocking the ledger to the floor.

"One moment," roared the pimp. "I am not a violent man, but I suggest you sit down and calm yourself before you get hurt...again." From one of the tables Maximilian appeared, sweeping behind David and ushering him back into his seat. Then delicately, the giant knelt down and retrieved the ledger, placing it back on the table.

The slight commotion startled Teresa, who witnessed the incident along with the young man at the bar. Not wanting to expose her emotions any more than necessary, she quickly surmised that David was in no danger. Reluctantly she looked up at her nervous companion, and with a forced smile suggested they leave the cantina.

His emotions nearly depleted, David watched helplessly as the two left the bar. Unaware of Tito's scrutinizing gaze, David began vigorously massaging an aching temporal lobe. The therapy failed, and with the painful throbbing increasing, he glared pleadingly at Tito. "I've got to talk to her. She needs to know how I feel about her."

"I think she knows how you feel, señor, because she feels the same about you. I've sensed that since you were first in her care. She's changing, becoming more withdrawn and reflective. And I attribute that to her thinking about you."

David leaned in, nervously working the lower hinges of his jaw. "Then you must help me convince her to get out of this…this situation."

Tito offered an abbreviated snicker and pressed his generous girth against the chair. "You know my niece by now. There is nothing I can do or say to dissuade her. She has a goal in mind, and intends to achieve it. At least that's been her thinking up to now.

"Look, Señor David," the pimp continued, fanning his Panama. "You know I am no more happy about this than you are. I'd love to see her find a good man like yourself, settle down, and have babies. But until that time, if this is what she wants, I'd rather she do it working for me than for some blood sucking pimp in Acapulco."

Tito halted his fanning and looked furtively around the room, as if someone might be listening. "I know several of these swine," he whispered, crossing himself. "Unspeakably evil, the way they treat their women. Why, did you know…?" He stopped suddenly, reading the depressive features of the American. "Oh, never mind, it's not important." Tito sat quietly for a moment, troubled by the actions of his new friend and feeling guilty at his own garrulous squawking.

After some thought he opened his ledger, rotating

47

it in front of David. "Hmmm," he murmured, stroking his thick, black mustache. "I see Teresa will be off this evening. Why don't you return to your home, and I'll see if I can arrange for her to meet you there, say about 9:00? I think this would be a civilized hour for both of us. Do you have any objections to the time?"

David's head bolted upwards, his expression childlike. "Do you think she'll come, señor?"

Calming David with his most avuncular look, Tito nodded forcefully. "Of course she will. I'm known to be very persuasive."

"Fantastic," blurted David. He clutched the older man's hand and pumped it vigorously, inadvertently crushing Tito's Panama in the process. "Tito, I'm so sorry. I—"

"Don't worry about it, young man," the pimp interrupted. "That's the beauty of Panama hats. Like the perfect woman, it never loses its shape, no matter what. Now, go on home. I know you have much to do."

David sprinted all the way from the cantina, arriving home out of breath. Within seconds he was rummaging about the rooms, picking up soiled clothes, emptying the trash, and throwing three-day-old dirty dishes into a tub of hot, soapy water. After a hasty dance with the vacuum cleaner, he removed a six-year-old bottle of California cabernet, which he'd been saving, from his study. Opening the wine, David let it breathe, allowing him enough time to shower, dress, and crank up an old phonograph that he'd stacked with classical records.

He'd completed everything he had to do in record time, and now sat at the edge of the couch, naked at the waist, rearranging the magazines on his coffee table. Judging one as being too risqué for company, David quickly whisked it under his feet, thankful for the inch high clearance beneath him. As the place began looking marginally civilized, David took a minute to compose himself, then got up to retrieve his shirt. He got as far as the bedroom when there came a firm knock on the door.

She's here, he thought impulsively, racing through the foyer clutching his shirt. David placed a clammy hand on the brass knob, counted to ten, then calmly opened the door. The reserved visage of Teresa clad in her simple, white cotton dress met the bare chested American.

"Hello, Señor Sherr...er...David," she offered.

"Hello, Teresa. I'm glad you were able to come."

"Yes, I can see that." Teresa's eyes moved downward toward David's tanned chest. "So this is how you present yourself to your female guests?" she teased.

"Oh, Jesus," he said with a prominent blush, only now realizing he wasn't wearing a shirt. "I'm sorry. Just got out of the shower." David retreated a step back into the interior of the foyer and dressed.

The young woman followed him, her lilac-scented moves carrying her into the living room. Teresa spotted a tattered, wicker chair positioned opposite the couch and sat down.

"Nicely furnished," she said, continuing her playful dialogue. "I guess you favor the minimalist look that I see in all the American art magazines."

A wry smile emerged from David. Surveying the room, he realized for the first time just how Spartan his surroundings were. "Never been much for material things," he countered. "Just ask my ex-wife."

Seeing that Teresa had been made comfortable, David excused himself to retrieve their drinks. When he emerged carrying two large goblets of wine, David noticed Teresa had moved to the living room window, where she peered down at the village. She stood with her back to David, unaware that he had re-entered the room: her pose, almost regal in design; her black hair flowing downward to the small of her back.

For a slight second David considered sliding a hand around her waist, but vetoed the idea, remembering to keep a neutral perspective. Instead, David quietly moved to her side and gazed out of the window as well. "It's really beautiful, this little town of yours."

"Yes," she sighed, continuing her study of the village from afar.

Teresa's preoccupation afforded David the opportunity to more fully scrutinize the Mexican beauty. He could smell her sweet breath, which he swore quickened as he brushed near her. With some hesitancy, Teresa turned obliquely toward the American. David sensed she was about to say something, when instead she cleared her throat and took a half step back, her demeanor noticeably changed.

"Uncle Tito suggested I check on you. He said you're

still not fully recovered from your wound."

The nape of David's neck bristled with anger. *Is this why she came?*

"Well, you needn't worry, I'm fine." David cursed inwardly at himself, sensing the haughtiness of his words. Teresa, too, recognized the indifference of her own remarks and reached for his hand. Drawing closer, she cautiously placed her head on his chest.

"David, that's not why I'm here. I wanted to come sooner, but.... I couldn't, I just couldn't."

Completely caught off guard by Teresa's emotional confession, David struggled to maintain his own composure. On impulse, he placed a palm to her cheek and kissed her.

"I know you find what I do distasteful," she said shakily. "Whenever I see you, there is always that look of disappointment, and I can't bear — "

Again David kissed her, this time deeper, more passionately. She closed her eyes, relinquishing the burden of her frustrations to the comforting strength of David's arms. But Teresa's conscience shortened the moment. She drew back, holding his wrists at arm's length.

"Please, David, I must finish. I haven't come to see you because I don't want to see you hurt. I wish I could make you understand."

She sucked in her breath and stared longingly at David through watery eyes. David, for his part, had never seen her so vulnerable and disconsolate. Selfishly, he took this as a good omen, recalling Tito's comment that the

American was getting to her. Bolstered by this newfound confidence, David scooped up the slender woman and carried her to his bed.

***

They made love late into the night, pausing for an occasional respite before resuming their passions. David became the aggressor, using an indolent hand to inch his fingers over the contours of her flattened stomach. The tips of each digit flowed lightly over soft down that aligned itself with her coarser, moist pubic hairs. Reversing direction, he then snaked upward to her breasts and feathered the pinkish nipples with a flickering pass. Teresa moaned, removing the hand from her breast and thrust the offending finger into her mouth, suckling it voraciously.

"Mmmm, you taste good," she growled.

"So do you," said David.

He recalled their initial session only a few hours earlier when he'd placed her on the bed, removed her dress and panties, and submerged himself on her awaiting body. The descent had been ecstasy for David, traveling from lips to breasts to navel to, finally, her inner thighs. Eagerly, Teresa had parted her legs and watched, transfixed, as David sought out the dank interiors of her unveiled furrow with his tongue before mounting her. Driven to exhaustion, the lovers slept soundly, unaware of the morning sun that swept into the room, casting a golden hue over them.

***

David shifted lazily, blinking a few times before

prying open an eye. Two larger eyes stared back.

"How ya' doing?" he asked.

Teresa emitted a contented yawn and cooed, "I feel wonderful."

He rolled onto his back and faced the ceiling, his hands latched behind his head. "And how did I do?" David wanted his comment to come across as frivolous, although his ego begged a positive evaluation from his lover. Teresa giggled and pushed herself nearer David, kissing the corners of his mouth with a teasing tongue.

"You were magnificent, David, really. I've never experienced such…such heat."

David's Adam's apple fluctuated and he swallowed hard, fighting off the temptation to jump out of bed and dance a jig. Even though he'd had his share of women over the years, David always felt so alive and functional whenever he was in her company. It thrilled him to be able to feel like that again — to feel life rekindling.

An hour later, the two sat at the kitchen table drinking coffee and finishing off an omelet breakfast Teresa had prepared. They talked of many things: the village, politics, nursing, their families, everything but her job. David even suggested they go away for a weekend, which caught Teresa by surprise.

Shortly afterward, Teresa said she needed to get back to the cantina to help Tito with the books. David acceded without incident, even allowing a tiny smile to cross his face. As he walked her to the door, he asked her again about a weekend getaway.

Teresa paused in calculation. "How about next weekend? I'm sure my uncle won't mind. Would that be all right with you?"

"That would be perfect," he beamed. "I'll book us in Acapulco's swankiest hotel, or at least one with clean sheets, and we'll spend two days playing the role of the idle rich. How does that sound?"

Teresa doubled over with laughter, covering her face in her hands. "You are one crazy gringo."

CHAPTER FIVE

The week was full, just the way David wanted it. He was obviously ecstatic about his escape with Teresa, but thankful that his job kept him focused. There'd be plenty of time to think about Teresa, and that excited him greatly.

As with all small towns, it was impossible to hide secrets for long in Mancha Negra. David's students had by now developed genuine feelings for him. Additionally, they had heard of his growing relationship with the young prostitute. They waited all week until Friday's dismissal and, instead of vacating the tiny classroom, surrounded the puzzled teacher at his desk.

Jaime Reyes stepped forward from the encircled group, and without speaking, presented David with a small, neatly wrapped gift.

"Please, open it, Señor Sherry," another student requested.

David obliged, still unsure of what was happening. Removing the last of the stuffed tissue, he pulled out a copper bracelet with inlaid stones of mother of pearl. "I don't understand. I—"

"Señor Sherry," explained Jaime. "This is a gift of love. Many years ago, as our fathers have told us and their fathers to them, there lived in this area the Tzentál, an ancient Indian tribe who were known for their ornate copper works. This type of bracelet had great significance to them. When the time was right, a Tzentál tribesman would place the bracelet on the wrist of his woman, so others would know she was betrothed to him. In the smaller mountain villages this practice continues, even now. We thought that.... Well, that you might have someone special who'd appreciate receiving this replica." Titters erupted among several of the students.

Their teacher's face reddened. David knew it would be useless to feign innocence. Besides, he was genuinely touched by their concern and generosity. "I don't know what to say except thank you. And if, by chance, there is someone special in my life, perhaps after this weekend she may be enticed to wear this bracelet."

Bellowing their approval, the students gathered even closer to David, shaking his hand and wishing him good luck before they departed from school.

"See you on Monday, Señor Sherry," cheered Carlos, his youngest student, and the last to leave.

David got up and walked to a corner of his desk, where he sat, his legs dangling over the edge. He picked up the bracelet, rubbed his thumb over the smooth copper finish, and then moved it to his other hand, bouncing it in his palm to determine its weight. *Must have cost those kids quite a bit, replica or not,* he pondered. David continued to study the gift, bemused, as he thought of Jaime's words. "To be placed on the wrist of his betrothed."

***

With an arm stretched out beyond the padded headrest of the passenger seat, David thumped his fingers rhythmically and waited for Teresa. He looked again at the tiny back seat and made sure his suitcase was secure. The Jeep could hold plenty of luggage, at least that's what Roberto Lopez had told him. The little Mexican, the first person to befriend him upon his arrival, had loaned him the Jeep for the weekend. He, too, had heard the rumors of a tryst between his American employee and Teresa, and was more than willing to be of service.

Seven-forty. He was twenty minutes early. The sun was still well above the horizon, although shadowy lines began flooding the narrow alleys. David turned on the car radio and thumbed through the a.m. band. Midway through his searching he picked up some American rock-and-roll from a station in Acapulco and joined in, crooning to the sounds of the Beach Boys. Before realizing it, twenty minutes had elapsed; by the time he rechecked his watch, David discovered there was no longer enough light to read it. He shifted uneasily in his seat and began unrolling his window when he heard the passenger door open.

"Hello, David," Teresa breathlessly exclaimed. "Did you miss me?" Turning her back to him, Teresa reached down and brought up a stuffed, imitation brown leather overnight bag, which she tossed on top of David's. She looked at him in mock exasperation. "Well, I'm waiting for an answer."

"You bet I did." David leaned to his right, kissing her deeply. "I was counting the minutes. All set?"

"I will be in two minutes. I just need to tell Lucy she can use my house tonight when she's through with work."

"Why does she need to do that?" David asked.

"Well, it's probably nothing, but Lucy thinks a man has been shadowing her the past couple of days. Twice someone followed her home; once after she'd visited a friend's house, and later as she left the Club El Gato. She couldn't make out who it was, because he always kept his distance and walked on the other side of the street."

"Is she sure he followed her home?" David's interest began to pique.

"Yes, of course. After Lucy got home she looked through the curtains, and saw him leaning against a wall staring in her direction."

"And she couldn't make out who it was?" David continued.

"No, it was too dark. She did notice he was doing something with his hands, like holding one still while seeming to strike it with the other. Sort of like—how do you say? Whittling."

"Whittling?" exclaimed David. "You mean carving with a knife?"

"Si, that's what I mean. Anyway, Lucy now thinks it was just a drunken villager, or maybe an artisan she met from the cantina who's enamored with her. He seemed to hang around for a few minutes on both occasions, then went away. It's probably nothing, but she doesn't want to take any chances. I'm sure you agree."

"Does she live with anybody?"

"Her mother," replied Teresa. "But she's in Durango right now visiting Lucy's grandmother, who's not well. She'll be back in a couple of days. Anyway, I thought that since I'm going to be gone, Lucy can use my house just as a precaution."

David nodded his head in agreement. "Sounds good to me. Better go tell her, but hurry back."

Blowing him a kiss and winking slyly, Teresa sprinted around the corner and vanished in an instant, echoing the faint sound of high heels on the paved alleyway.

Her allotted two minutes passed. In fact, more than ten minutes had gone by since Teresa excused herself and darted out of the Jeep.

"What's wrong now?" David grumbled. He managed to constrain himself for another few seconds before deciding to see what was going on. Leaving the Jeep, David traced Teresa's steps beyond the cantina to the corner alley. He'd never been down this street before, but felt an instant distaste for what he saw.

On both sides of the semi-circle shaped street were eight evenly spaced one-room wooden dwellings. To David's way of thinking they were no more than hovels, with their windowless pinkish walls and plywood doors. They reminded him of the motels he'd seen along Route 66 as a kid while traveling across the southwest with his family.

The distasteful image of Teresa lying with another man in one of those shacks altered his stride a bit. He stopped and cleared his head, releasing the demons, then continued. Amid the darkness David heard the creaking of a partially opened door. He moved haltingly in the direction of the sound and poked his head into the obscure quarters.

"Hello, Teresa. You in here?" There seemed to be no sound and, as he turned to go, David heard what he thought was snickering coming from within the room. He extended himself even farther inside and saw a hazy figure of a naked woman lying on a bed, legs spread apart and bent at the knees. Although the face was encased in shadow, David caught sight of a glistening pair of white teeth that flashed and darkened, again and again, caught by the cantina's garish neon lighting, which beckoned overhead from a corner wing.

"Why you little tease," admonished David, unveiling a salacious smile and feeling strangely excited by this impromptu liaison. "I should have known something was up after that crazy wink of yours." He closed the door behind him, swallowing up the blinking yellow phosphorescence of the cantina's sign. In a loud, dramatic voice he said, "Well, I wonder where Teresa could possibly be?" He began inching his way in the general path of the bed, homing in on the stillness of that remarkably glossy smile he'd seen moments ago.

Reaching the bed, David stood over the silent woman, the overwhelming scent of perfume permeating his nostrils.

"My, my, what do we have here?" The woman remained mute, unperturbed by David's emoting display. David bent forward, arching himself only inches away from the woman's lips. But a suppressed murmur from across the room froze the lanky American. Instantly, David jerked back and peered into the recesses of the room, searching for the source of that sound.

"Who's there?" David spoke softly, his voice struggling to extract a confident volume. That snickering sound again, he thought. Or was it? David held his breath, straining to hear any additional disturbances, forgetting altogether the image on the bed. *Yesss*, he assumed more assuredly, *there it is again*. Only this time it was louder and seemed to be coming from the opposite corner. *Jesus*, David concluded. *That's no snicker, that's a sob. Someone's crying.*

Again he called out, but this time the crying stopped. With his mind racing, it suddenly occurred to David that he'd been barking out his demands in English. As calmly as he could, David repeated, "*Quien Es?*" This proved equally unsuccessful, so he continued to wait, staring into the black void for some reaction. When none came David decided to move toward the wall closest to him, hoping that somewhere nearby he'd find a light switch. He groped along the way, patting the wall in large sweeping circles. "Dammit," he said. "Where's that fucking switch?"

David reversed direction, frantically hoping to find a light over the bed. "C'mon, c'mon. It's got to be here." His leg hit the edge of a protruding mattress, which jackknifed him into the headboard. Struggling to correct his fall, his fingers brushed a plastic rectangle beveled into the wall. The switch!

He'd found it, but as David flicked it upwards a cold hand touched his neck. The twenty-five watt bulb did little more than outline the shaken figure who draped itself into his arms before pushing the two of them onto the single bed.

"Teresa, what—?" David halted in mid-sentence, staring at the saucer-like eyes that appeared to look beyond him. With wild abandon she struggled to free herself from David, shoving at him with outstretched arms. He held on, attempting to disarm her fury, while gently pulling her toward him. It was then that David remembered the huddled form lying next to him.

Lucy's eerie, unwavering smile greeted him, paralyzing his efforts to flee. He remembered her as the girl Vega had challenged on the dance floor. In stunned repugnance, David surveyed the corpse's gaudy expression. Someone had surgically removed her upper and lower lips, exposing a set of white-veined gums and bloodied canines. Dried strips of bloodied skin resembling a mustache ran from under her septum to her ear lobes. Three additional pieces of skin dangled from her chin. Yet her body showed no signs of struggle throughout the ordeal, her head braced and slightly elevated, her legs locked in their provocative stance.

In slow, deliberate movements the two lovers extricated themselves from the supine body, back pedaling to the foot of the bed. David fought to suppress the rising bile in his throat.

"David, look, do you see it?" Teresa shrieked. David's mouth dropped, disgust giving way to surprise. From the position in which he stood he could now see the real cause of Lucy's death: an eight-inch slash carved evenly across her throat.

They'd seen enough. David and Teresa lumbered out of the room into the cool, dry night, where they stood inhaling gulps of clean, tropical air. David looked wearily at Teresa, who'd stepped off the curb and crouched down on her haunches, whimpering silently to herself.

He approached her and gently called out her name, but Teresa didn't respond. Her head bobbed up and down and she began to speak with some clarity, although it wasn't David she was talking to. When he'd heard enough of the conversation he tenderly intervened, placing a compassionate arm around Teresa. "You and I need to take a walk." And together they crossed through the plaza to the tiny police station.

***

For nearly three hours David and Teresa sat, numbly describing what they'd seen and answering questions being asked of them by Sergeant Virgilio Arroyo. Initially David did most of the talking, as the glassy-eyed Teresa stared vacuously at the two men, offering an occasional mutter of affirmation or denial. She'd ceased her one-way conversation with the dead girl, and slowly began gaining control of her emotions. Arroyo seemed sensitive to her condition, and did little to press her for answers.

Arroyo was a reed-thin man of fifty-five. His sparse brown hair was parted near the top of his right ear and pulled over his scalp, where he'd puffed it up for purposes of height. David thought it resembled a rogue wave caught by a still camera. The sergeant sat with his feet up on his desk, copiously taking notes with the stub of a number two pencil.

Earlier, Arroyo had sent out his only officer, Muela, to substantiate their story; when he returned ashen faced and shaken, Arroyo got his answer. The sergeant rose from his desk and walked over to his subordinate, eyeing him curiously. He whispered something into the man's ear. Muela tensed, quelling the urge to protest, then stammered, "Sí Sergente, I understand."

All three watched as Officer Muela scurried about the office, first moving to a large, army green locker, from which he extracted a Polaroid camera, and then to his desk, where he removed a crude fingerprinting kit. Placing the equipment in a small plastic bag, he bolted to the door, glancing furtively at his superior.

"Eduardo," warned Arroyo, "remember to take your time. When you are done get Señor Alvarez to seal off that room, then take the evidence to state headquarters in Chilpancingo. I will arrange for the coroner at Iguala to pick up the body. Comprende?"

Muelo swallowed hard. "Sí, señor."

As the door closed, the sergeant ended the questioning and sidled over to the couple, extending his hand to David. "I'm sorry you two had to come to me under these circumstances. Teresa, I know Lucy was a good friend of yours, and we'll do all we can to find out who did this." Directing his final statements to David, he added, "Things of this nature are very rare in Mancha Negra. For the thirteen years I've been sergeant here, we've never had a murder. In fact, the last person here to die violently was.... Let's see. Yes, the German artist in whose house you're now living. Isn't that right, Teresa?"

Both men looked questioningly at the saddened Mexicana, who peered sheepishly at them, offering Arroyo a faint nod. Exhaustion shrouded her face, and she fought back the painful images of that evening. Mustering up her reserves, she spoke. "And now, Sergeant, if you don't mind I'd like to go home."

"Certainly," he replied. "You both are free to go. I'm sorry I had to put you through this ordeal. Good night, and thank you for all your cooperation."

It was a few minutes past midnight when David and Teresa left the building and walked to the Jeep. They drove silently back to David's house, too fatigued to worry about bringing in the packed suitcases that lay piled on the backseat.

Lying in bed, encircled in one another's arms, restless thoughts encumbered their sleep.

David whispered. "You awake?"

"Yes"

"Remember during the questioning when the sergeant asked if you knew of anyone who might have wanted to cause Lucy harm, and you said no?"

"Yes, so?"

David withdrew his arm from under her neck and propped himself up on an elbow.

"Well, I was thinking. The night I had that fight in the Club El Gato, the man who swore at her—"

"Of course!" she interrupted, snapping her fingers. "What was his name again?"

"Vega, I believe."

Teresa sat up as well, pulling with her a blanket that she pressed to her chest. "After we had you taken to my house, you fell unconscious for nearly an hour. Lucy helped me clean your wound and, during that time, explained what had happened. She told me she'd been with this Vega earlier in the evening, and that he was one mean drunk. Very loud and crude, I think she said. He kept asking her personal questions, which she refused to answer. She said he bought her for a second hour, but by the time Vega crawled into bed and got on top of her, he passed out. Lucy rolled him over, got dressed, and came back to the cantina. It probably wasn't more than an hour later that your run in with him occurred."

David leapt from the bed. "You stay here. I'm going back to talk to the sergeant. I'll bet between Tito and myself we can come up with a pretty good description of this Vega character."

In a doleful, almost pleading look, Teresa moved back the sheets and patted the bed.

"Please, David, can't this wait until tomorrow morning? I don't want to be alone right now. I need you here with me."

He considered her offer and smiled longingly. Even without makeup, and with unkempt hair and puffy eyes, Teresa couldn't have been lovelier, he thought. "Yeah, sure, it can wait. Besides, I really didn't want to be the guy who has to wake Tito up at this hour."

David slipped back under the covers, placing his arm around Teresa. The heat of his warm body drew her close. She emitted a soft drone, thanking him for staying, but David never heard. Content nonetheless, she listened to the cadenced snores of her lover.

***

Ramon Vega could stand the stench no longer. Hunched inside the mouth of Mancha Negra's ancient sewer system, he watched the final throes of light dip into the Pacific Ocean. Stagnant water reeking of human waste and decaying algae churned with his slightest movement. Granted, this repulsive, cement orifice had provided Vega nearly twenty-four hours of refuge, but it was time to move on. He felt certain the police had halted their search by now. Breaking from his crouch, Vega stretched and shuffled toward the opening, following the overflow of seepage that spewed out over a small embankment and into the sea.

Dropping to his hands and knees to exit the sewer pipe, he heard the distinct plopping sound of metal hitting water, and knew immediately what had fallen from his pocket. Vega held his breath as he plunged a hand into the murky swell, extracting the piece of jewelry by its gold

67

chain. He rubbed a thumb over the outer casing of the locket, ridding it of a clump of sludge and then popped open the clasp. Vega gazed at the faded photo of what he assumed was Lucy's mother. Despite the pallid luster, Vega's good eye bore hard at the heavily jowled cheeks and open-mouthed smile, the latter feature carelessly glossed in thick shades of red.

This was a feature Vega knew all too well. He could almost hear the insidious brand of laughter that accompanied that look. Such a mocking combination had infested his soul for much of his life, beginning with his mother.

***

Little Ramon had lived with his mother and younger brother in an Acapulco slum far from the glitzy tourist shops and pink, sandy beaches. Large cardboard strips taped together divided the one room shanty, segregating him and six-year-old Miguelito from their mother and the numerous "uncles" who came and left on a daily basis.

The tiny children were given two basic rules: be very quiet and stay out of the way. Both knew that to make even the slightest sounds while their mother was entertaining was to warrant a vicious beating. Once, when Ramon was battling a bout of diarrhea, he had relieved himself in his shorts, too afraid to call out to his mother for help. Gradually the objectionable stench reached the other side of the partition, where their mother and a grizzled Mexican sailor were in the midst of lovemaking.

"*Madre De Díos!*" exclaimed the sailor. "What is that

smell?"

Ramon reached out for his sibling, placing a hand over his brother's mouth. He knew that at any moment there'd be angry movements coming from the other side of the room. With his eyes shut tightly, he waited for the living nightmare to begin.

"This is too much to bear, woman. The deal is off."

The children heard the rustling of clothing followed by their mother's voice.

"Wait, don't go. I can—"

"You can't do shit," the sailor interrupted. "I'm going to throw up if I don't get out of here. Now, out of my way."

The boys' mother offered a remorseful hand, but the sailor pushed her back with an indignant shove to her chest. She fell, tumbling over the cardboard partition and sprawling face down at the feet of her sons.

With the sailor gone, everything in the room remained motionless for what seemed like an eternity to the two children. Then, with an ungainly, almost reptilian twist of her torso, the woman turned to face Ramon. Heavily mascaraed eyes produced a pair of black, wavy droplets, which streaked down her face. She resembled a snarling dog with yellowish teeth, enclosed by bloated and ill-formed pink lips. Ramon noticed a slight cut on her lower lip, which had already begun coagulating. For some reason it pleased him enormously to see her in such a wretched state of discomfort, but he knew better than to exhibit such feelings in her presence.

Too drunk or weak to stand, the woman began

crawling on all fours, her sagging, naked breasts skimming the dingy floor. She neared the older boy, pulling him by the leg and straddling him. Young Miguelito drew a short breath and placed his hands over his eyes. Ignoring him, she sighted directly down at the Ramon.

"I'll bet you're the one who ruined my night, eh, you little bastard?" Lowering her eyes to his crotch, she spied a dark stream of fecal matter extending beyond his underpants. Angrily she thrust her slender, blue-veined hand under his chin and pulled him even closer to her. So close in fact that the image she presented was of something abstract; a cubist meshing of lines and colors diluted with the smell of cheap tequila.

Extending the slightest resistance to his mother's hold, he managed to free himself from her grasp. With her position already tenuous, the move was just forceful enough to break her balance and drive her face straight down to his. Distorted obscenities rang from the half-hidden mouth, and as Ramon attempted to push himself free of her, a vicious clamping of teeth seized hard on his chin, eliciting a pain of unfathomable proportions.

Luckily for Ramon, the incident itself was cut short. The woman's drunken condition soon drew her into the realm of unconsciousness. Summoning up all his strength, the boy pushed her aside, his tiny chest heaving against her weight. After a moment's respite, he tended to his own wounds, dabbing his tongue at a patch of blood which clung to his chin.

Despite his youth, Ramon concluded that his injuries

were not serious and turned his attention to his brother, who returned his stare with vacant eyes. They'd witnessed these tirades before, and knew they'd experience them again. Ramon ran a hand over Miguelito's hair.

"Someday, little brother, we're going to get out of here and leave her to her stinking...uncles. You'll see."

***

The locket sifted through Vega's fingers, plummeting again into the brackish stream. He stooped to pick it up, then thought better of it. "A perfect place for you and your kind. May you rot here forever."

Images of last night's carnage remained fresh in his mind and, as much as he would have enjoyed reflecting on the events of Lucy's murder, he needed to move on. Vega peeked his head out of the sewer opening and drew in a deep, cleansing breath. Stratus clouds shadowed a gibbous moon, affording him enough light by which to travel.

Crossing over a stretch of two lane road, Vega trekked eastward, directing himself along the jungle. Climbing higher near the tree line, he paused to catch his breath and gazed down on the tiny, lit community of Mancha Negra.

A self-assured jaw protruded from under an angry smirk. "Alvarez, you and that whoring brood of yours have not seen the last of Ramon Vega."

Chapter Six

It was early afternoon before David eased himself out of bed. He dressed without showering, slipped out the door, and headed for the police station. Teresa continued to doze, her torment finally giving way to deep slumber.

Finding Sergeant Arroyo, David gave him the information and suggested he also contact Tito. Afterwards, he decided that while in town he'd go over to the bakery and bring back some items for himself and Teresa. David was ravenous at this point, appreciative that his appetite was returning and hoping Teresa's was as well.

Crossing the street, he made his way to the pandaria. A small cowbell clanged as he opened the door. The proprietor, Señor Felipe Duran, stood facing him, keys in his hand. "*Lo siento, señor,* but I will be closing for one hour. News about Lucy has reached our village, so we're going to church for a special mass."

David nodded respectfully to Duran and left the tiny shop. He stood in front of a nearby pharmacy and watched the man step from the sidewalk into the street, where he was met by his wife and another couple. Together they trudged up the road to church. Arriving home twenty minutes later, David heard stirrings in the bedroom. Teresa entered the living room and plopped down on the couch, resting her feet on the coffee table.

"Hi," he said.

"Hello," came a lazy response.

"Feeling better?"

"Yes, a little." Teresa rubbed the sleep from her eyes. "Did you see Arroyo?"

"Uh huh. I told him what I knew. He was on his way to meet Tito when I left his office." David helped her to her feet and stood back in admiration, watching Teresa go through the sensual contortions of an early morning stretch.

"You hungry?" queried David.

"Umm. A little."

"Good, I'll make us some French toast. I tried buying some pastries from Señor Duran, but he was closing just as I got there. He said they were holding some sort of mass for Lucy—"

"Dear Jesus," she gasped. "I must go. We must go!"

"But don't you want to eat some—?"

"Please, let's hurry, David." Teresa flew into the bedroom, where she'd threw on her clothes and slid into her sandals. David waited for her outside the door, patiently jangling car keys in one hand while gulping down cold coffee with the other.

Within minutes they'd reached the church, parking the Jeep just steps from the arched entrance way. They could hear the priest's muffled promptings, followed by a harmonial return from the small congregation. David and Teresa sidled unobtrusively along the back wall behind the confessional until they caught sight of Tito, who, with his customary Panama hat, beckoned them forward.

Together they listened to the priest's eulogy, with Teresa genuflexed in prayer and flanked by the two men. David, long an agnostic and frustrated by the impotence of organized religion, did his best to keep still while Tito's focus centered on the welfare of his niece.

He cast his sunken eyes down on her and then turned toward David. Although Tito didn't speak, David could read the apprehension etched on the pimp's pleading face. Yes, David reflected, *I will take good care of Teresa and protect her just as you have. You can count on this, my friend.*

At the front of the congregation, elevated high in his pulpit, the robed clergyman continued, his palms outstretched and facing the heavens. "The Lord knoweth the days of them that are whole-hearted, and their inheritance shall be forever...."

***

The two lovers remained nearly inseparable for the rest of the weekend. With their relationship in its early stages, they'd already shared enough grief and knocked down enough barriers between them to last a lifetime. David had made a conscious effort to suppress any ill-conceived comments regarding Teresa's professional life. Teresa countered by openly talking about the day she'd be able to leave this oldest of professions for what David had earlier referred to as "legit work."

The only obstacle was meeting a timetable. The young prostitute had estimated that by early summer she'd be debt free, although the possibility of returning to nursing school would be out of the question; that would require another eighteen months spent on her back. She knew David would never be able to handle it.

Alone in the shower after they'd made love, Teresa contemplated her dilemma. Maybe it isn't so damned important to get a nursing degree, she posed. Before David, she was alone and searching for a purpose; but now that David had entered the picture, priorities had shifted. Was marriage a possibility? Could they settle down here in Mancha Negra?

Would David be able to accept her as an ex-prostitute? Teresa drew a forefinger to her lips, as if to stifle such frivolous thoughts and, in doing so, felt the heavy copper bracelet dangling on her wrist. She smiled, eyeing the cool, metallic gift, and clutched it to her bosom.

After David left for work the next morning, Teresa returned to her job. She told a surprised Tito she wanted to cut back her hours in order to spend more time with the American. However, she still insisted on working the peak money-making shifts: Friday and Saturday evenings. Her uncle, hoping to hear that she was quitting altogether, reluctantly agreed.

Teresa then returned to David's house and left him a note, directing him to meet her at the cantina at about ten that evening. She didn't indicate why, other than to say it was the start of some good news.

At precisely that hour Teresa said goodbye to her last client and left her little cubicle for the cantina. Entering through the rear exit, she found David sitting with Tito at the pimp's customary corner seat, engaged in some lengthy discussion.

Poor David, thought Teresa. *He seems like a student himself, always so serious and attentive to Tito. And my uncle, so flattered by it all. God, how I love them both.*

Teresa approached, greeting each man with a kiss to the cheek. "Sorry we can't stay, Tito, but I have something I need to say to David. Do you mind?"

The pimp pushed a limp hand toward them. "Of course I don't mind. I know you two have a lot to talk about." He walked the couple to the door, engaging them in small talk, then bid them good evening before returning to his table.

The two lovers sauntered into the plaza and sat down on a park bench, snuggling against the late night chill. Teresa removed a tissue from a pocket and dabbed her nose. "Thank you for coming," she said, sniffling.

"What's this good news you wrote about?"

"Well, uh.... I wanted you to know that I'm going to be working fewer hours at the Club El Gato."

David lifted an eyebrow. "You mean you're leaving the business?"

"No. I said I'm cutting back, not quitting. That way we can spend more time together. You want that, don't you?"

"Uh...sure," he replied in masked disappointment.

"Good, I was hoping you'd say that." Playfully poking at his ribs, Teresa sprung from the bench and pulled him up with her. "C'mon, let's go to my place. I can't wait to get you indoors."

***

Tito was enjoying himself. He loved to cook, but rarely had the time or found the occasion to do so. *How long has it been since my last bash? Eight months? Ten months?*

Yes of course, he recalled, *Fat Mata's combination engagement and going away party.* It had been over a year since Tito had thrown that bittersweet party for Mata Hernandez, the oldest of his regular girls.

Checking his watch, Tito noted that his guests wouldn't be arriving for another twenty minutes or so. He'd prepared well. The steaks had been marinating in their own juices for hours. Ten pounds of chorizo lay on the mesquite grill, spitting and popping from their casings. He expertly turned over the sausages, fanning the spiraling smoke with his chapeau. Tito stared into the haze and watched pensively as grey vapors dissipated into the evening sky.

He thought of Fat Mata. Despite the time that had elapsed since he last saw her, Tito recalled that final occasion with utter delight. Proudly he had greeted Mata and her fiancé at his seaside residence, escorting them to his capacious patio. A phalanx of honey-scented flowers and beautifully manicured bushes surrounded the couple and their guests. Father Gomez approached them, bestowing his blessings on their upcoming marriage. Tito held back a bit, ever the proverbial abandoned father whenever one of his girls left his employ to marry.

From out of the crowd came the cheerful chords of Pepe, the bartender's accordion, lifting Tito's sullen mood. Soon lost in the moment, Tito eagerly awaited his turn to dance with Mata, adding himself to the circle of other expectant men. One by one they'd release themselves from the ring and twirl her about before passing her to the next man.

When they'd reached the final dancer, the circle opened and Tito entered. Fat Mata pranced about deliriously and, using the crook of her index finger, enticed him deeper inside the ring. Everyone cheered as Tito sprung forward, his enormous frame surprisingly nimble.

The music faded under the raucous merriment of the guests, but the duo continued to dance, spinning about from one end of the garden to the next. After several minutes Tito's face was coated with sweat, and more than once someone had to reach out and right the wobbling dancer. Finally, the old pimp could dance no more. He backed off, bowing gracefully to both Mata and his bedazzled guests.

Festivities continued for the rest of the night until food, drink, and good times had eventually overtaken the guests. In increments of twos and threes they retreated to their respective homes. Fata Mata and her fiancé were the last to leave. With a look of sadness the woman embraced her old boss for a final time. "I'll never forget you, Tito. You've cared for me like no one else ever has."

Uncomfortable with Fat Mata's outpouring of emotion, Tito stepped out of her embrace and feigned an itch near the corner of his eye. "Damned mosquitoes, they're everywhere this time of year," he said. "Ah.... Er.... Listen, Mata, you're going to be just fine. Frankie seems like a nice young man."

As if on cue Frankie embraced her, guiding his hand to her shoulder. He could feel an underlying tension from beneath her heavy sweater. Together they moved along the front path to their car. As Frankie opened the passenger door, Fata Mata turned again and waved farewell.

"Goodbye, Mata," Tito mouthed. "Have a good life."

Tito couldn't remember just how long he stood on the steps after they'd gone. He was tired and felt the gout in his legs beginning to act up. A man of his size was not made for such dancing, but Fata Mata was worth the sacrifice. He pulled a cigar from his shirt but thought better of it. For now sleep was more important.

Tito received letters from Mata almost weekly, and it was the fourth letter that brought him the joyous news. She'd become pregnant. Tito relayed this news to others in Mancha Negra, and they all seemed to share in the happiness. Friends of Mata's pooled their money and sent her a brand new crib. Tito sweetened the pot by sending the newlyweds two hundred dollars.

The child was scheduled to be born near Christmas, and in fact, Tito received the call on Christmas Eve. He'd been suffering from the flu, and decided to leave the cantina early for some bedrest. The phone was ringing as he entered his home.

"Señor Alvarez, this is Frankie."

The pimp slid himself into a nearby chair, his misery forgotten. "Dear boy, how are you? How's Mata? Did you have the ba—?"

"Señor Alvarez, please. Mata is dead." There was a pause for a few seconds, and then the voice continued. "The doctors said it was massive bleeding. They could not control it. I…. I just wanted you to know. Señor Alvarez…. Senor Alvarez?"

The pimp needed only to hear of Mata's demise to prepare for what was about to happen. An involuntary fibrillation of aortic muscle seized his chest, pushing Tito back into the chair and forcing the phone into his lap. He sat, head down, drawing in soft, even breaths, willing away the pain he knew would only diminish with time. Tito had been through this routine before, and as such, continued to ignore the pernicious repercussions of his condition.

He picked up the phone, his voice heavy but calm. "I am here, Frankie."

"Are you okay, Tito?" Frankie asked.

The pimp ignored him, more concerned with his own inquiries. "Listen, Frankie, I must know. What about the child? Is the child all right?"

"Sí, jefe, the child is fine. I have a son…a son!"

"A son," Tito repeated to himself, his voice clearly weakened.

"Yes, and as healthy as a horse. Nine pounds, eight

ounces."

Frankie continued talking, but Tito heard little else. He tried to visualize the infant's features. A louder, more frustrated voice broke his concentration.

"Señor Alvarez, are you listening? As soon as everything calms down here, I will bring the child, your godchild, to Mancha Negra for a visit. Will that be okay with you?" Frankie waited patiently for a reply, unaware of Tito's labored attempts at recovery. Exasperated over the continued silence, the young man spoke again. "Goodbye, jefe, and God bless you. My son will know of your kindness."

A moment later the phone went dead. Tito, his hand still clutching the receiver, gently set it down. He never heard from Frankie or the child again.

Chapter Seven

"Uncle Tito, what are you trying to do, cremate the meat?" He recognized the voice of his niece, breaking his somber contemplations.

"*Perdone?*"

Teresa strolled up to him, noting his waxen features. "Is anything wrong? You seem distant."

"Goodness no, child. Everything is fine."

"Then why are you standing in the middle of all this smoke?" Teresa sniffed the air, wrinkling her nose. "Something's burning. Would you like a hand?"

"That's not necessary, thank you," Tito replied, slightly annoyed. "I can handle it." She knew this was not the time to push the issue, especially when it came to questioning her uncle's perceptions of Mexican cuisine. Granted, his dishes were generally burned beyond salvation, but few people felt comfortable enough to look him in the eye and tell him so. Coyly, Teresa withdrew without further comment, busying herself with other things.

Eyeing the meat for the first time, Tito swore under his breath. He grabbed a pair of tongs and snatched up two charred filets, hurling them in front of his two German shepherds lounging by the pathway leading to the garden. "Well," he said as he watched the hungry animals devour the steaks. "It's nice to see you two appreciate my cooking."

He reached behind the grill, removing a large plate filled with more steaks and sausages. Out of the corner of his eye Tito saw David enter the garden. The pimp smiled to himself, amused at the American's transformation. Gone were the penny loafers, his feet now donning local sandals. In place of his button-down oxfords was the bland white shirt of the *camposino*. Not wishing to disturb Tito, David had hung back near the entrance of the patio, sensing some disturbance with his host.

"Ah, Señor David, come, come. How nice you were able to accept my invitation." A fleshy hand grabbed David's. Teresa reappeared from the house and joined the men, offering each of them a glass of cold white wine.

"I can't stay and talk right now," she said. "Your maid, Ruby, is up to her neck in fruit salad, and has granted me a short reprieve. I must get back before I get into trouble.

David, why don't you help Uncle with the meat? It looks like he could use it." Enlivened at her own flippant commentary, Teresa chuckled to herself and rushed back into the house to assist Ruby.

"Aye, that woman," grumbled Tito with a shake of his head. "Just like her mother. Loves to tease."

When she'd gone, the men shifted over to the smoldering grill. David toyed with a spatula as Tito lifted an edge of the blackened grating and stoked the glowing, grey mesquite.

For the first time, David studied the grounds surrounding Tito's patio. "You've got quite a place here. How far are you from the beach?"

Tito clapped away the soot from his hands. "Oh, about fifty meters. Most people think I'm farther away than that because you can barely hear the waves." Tito pointed to the six-foot adobe walls surrounding the entire grounds. "I had them constructed especially for shutting out the ocean sounds."

The peculiarity of the pimp's statement drew a muddled stare from David.

"I know it sounds strange, Señor David, but hear me out. There is no doubt that I love the ocean. It's beautiful to look at. But to an insomniac like me, the perpetual sound of waves crashing upon rock, minute after minute, hour after hour, is an irritant for which there is no fit description."

Tito's haggard impression provoked a surge of laughter from both men, rendering them temporarily unaware of the guests that had begun making their way into the courtyard. The frivolity brought on a thirst which David attempted to quell with a long sip of wine. "Good stuff. Is this imported?"

"Yes, but this is merely a wine used to whet the pallet. I have some fine Chilean reds that I'll be introducing you to very soon. Are you a wine connoisseur?"

The American laughed. "Nope. I did try to drown my sorrows in it at one time, however."

84

Tito shot him an indifferent look. "We all handle grief in various ways. Why, just look at what Lucy's death has done to this village. It's been almost a month since she died, and many of her friends are still in mourning. It is time we stop and celebrate life. And what better way than to throw a party."

"Great idea. Besides, I'd like to meet more of Teresa's friends."

The pimp added a half dozen more chorizo to the grill. "You probably met most of them while you were recovering from that unfortunate incident. Let me tell you, they're all fine girls, whose only crime in life is that they were born poor with no one to give them direction. I would trust each of them with my life's belongings."

For an agonizing moment, David visualized his students back home, seeing them in Tito's description of his Mexican girls. It was that great equalizer—the need to survive—that excised whatever patience and innocence youth had provided them. He blanched at the memory of himself walking self-righteously out of the halls of Swann High that warm afternoon in June. David quickly drained the glass, hoping the wine would numb this distressing vision.

"Do you ever worry about all your girls eventually leaving?" asked David.

Tito cackled, his gelatinous belly rocking. "Leaving? No. Never. In poor pueblos like Mancha Negra, you'll always find some unfortunate waif desperate enough to sell her flesh to the highest bidder. An empty belly has no conscience."

"Ever had any problems with the girls?" David pursued.

The old pimp put a soot-stained forefinger to his cheek and thought for a minute. "I can honestly say that I've been quite lucky. I warn them beforehand that if they are dishonest in any way I'll send them packing. I explain to them the realities of this business. If they can accept it, fine. If not, then they should stay the hell out of it."

Without further comment Tito slapped a pair of tongs in David's hand and suggested he rotate the sausages on the grill. The American took that as the end of their conversation and complied.

"This calls for my special sauce. I've got a batch in the refrigerator." Throwing off his apron, Tito waddled into the house. He re-emerged a minute later, now accompanied by several guests, some of whom David had seen in town on other occasions.

To Tito's left walked Father Gomez, his mouth stuffed with a shrimp and cracker hors d'oeuvre. Behind him came Angie and Della Perez, two of Tito's girls. A rather tentative Sergeant Arroyo brought up the rear. The guests gathered around the grill while Tito made the introductions. Grabbing a spoon, he tapped it against a half-filled bottle of wine.

"Everyone, may I introduce my good friend, David Sherry. Señor David, I present to you Angie and Della Perez."

"Hello," said David, offering each his hand.

86

"*Con mucho gusto,*" came their joint replies.

Tito then turned to the priest. "And this is our most reverent Father Gomez. But I believe, Father, that you know David."

"Not formally," said the clergyman, extending his hand. "I've seen you about Mancha Negra, and know of your work with our children. I hear they're making great progress, thanks to you."

David, always uncomfortable when being praised, felt his face redden. "The children are very bright. They practically learn on their own."

Gomez smiled warmly. "Oh, I find that very hard to believe, Señor Sherry."

Catching sight of Sergeant Arroyo, Tito commented, "At least I'm sure you know this man."

"Sure," said David. "How are you?"

"Well, señor. And you?"

"I'm fine Sergeant, thank you. I haven't seen you since...well, since that night...with Lucy. Any progress on the case?"

***

Although he'd anticipated the question would arise during the course of the evening, Arroyo winced, and turned his gaze to Tito. He'd hoped to have been able to discuss the case with David alone, and not with the town's two most influential citizens listening in.

"No, Señor Sherry, not yet. I have received little information from headquarters. However, we're still interested in talking to the man you and Senõr Alvarez

87

described to us. If he's from one of the nearby coastal villages, we'll find him."

Arroyo's backhand wiped a line of perspiration forming on his upper lip. Tito said nothing, but continued to train his eyes on the man. In his youth, the pimp's temper had been legendary. Although the years had seemed to mellow Tito, the sergeant knew only too well the lengths to which Tito would go to protect those dear to him.

As a young patrolman, Arroyo had become engrossed with Tito's past. He'd read old police reports involving Tito's contraband liquor sales through Texas, and of his minor pimping misfortunes in San Luis, where he'd been known to sample the wares of his women. Once a jealous, unemployed husband of one of his whores had called him out into the streets, where they proceeded to pummel each other for over an hour. The fight ended with both men bloodied and driven to their knees. For Tito, the melee left him with a severely broken nose and a missing front tooth. Pepe, much smaller in stature, fared even worse: a separated shoulder and three busted ribs pushing against his lungs.

Few people who witnessed this exhibition realized how this incident came to affect the pimp. He had been in many brawls over the years, but never had Tito seen any man fight so valiantly to preserve a tenuous relationship with an adulterous wife. Overcome with guilt and fascinated by the broken man's commitment to his woman, Tito staggered toward the writhing Pepe and pulled him to his feet. They stood together in the middle of a dust-blown street, surrounded by a growing crowd of onlookers straining to hear the two men's conversation. The only audible words they could make out came from the bantam-weighted Pepe, who, while shaking Tito's hand, concluded, "Bartending suits me just fine. Thank you...boss."

From that point on Tito curtailed his carousing antics and made a conscious effort to refine his temper, as well as his personal life. Although there was still the occasional instance of rage, it would forever be limited to the defense of his girls.

The sergeant recalled well the last time he'd seen Tito unleash his bullish ire. According to the police report he'd filed — and had then made sure to misplace — the incident involved an aging Hollywood actor who'd ended up in the Club El Gato a few years back. Rex McKay strolled into the cantina after a day's filming a few miles south of Mancha Negra, and ended up drinking himself into a stupor. Witnesses claimed he pushed Fata Mata off her bar stool after she slapped him for groping her in public. Mata hit the floor, landing hard on her back. Her boss, who'd just entered the cantina, missed the entire incident, but one look at his beloved Mata told him what had happened. Tito was on the man at once, nearly choking him to death. It took three of Tito's best men to pull him away from the unconscious actor who, when later revived, hightailed it back to the States, refusing to complete the picture.

Sergeant Arroyo liked his job, and hoped he'd be notified of a lead regarding Lucy's murder soon. He was only five years short of retirement, but knew his pension was basically in the hands of Tito. There was no kidding himself. He was owned, body and soul, by the pimp. For the past two weeks the sergeant had gone to great lengths to avoid Tito, ordering Muela to take all phone calls while Arroyo was out patrolling Hornitos or Maldonaldo, the two sister villages within his district.

But tonight Arroyo had no choice. The giant Maximilian, under Tito's instructions, had gained access to the police station that morning, and when the sergeant opened up, there he stood.

"Senor Alvarez would like you to attend his party tonight at 7:00."

"I, uh…. Yes, with pleasure," Arroyo stammered.

With nothing further to say and his mission completed, Maximilian pushed past the sergeant, lowering his head as he passed through the doorway.

***

"I think it's time we all refreshed our drinks," suggested Father Gomez. "Tito, when are you going to break out the good stuff, eh?"

Tito paused a moment before answering with a slight tilt of his head, but his eyes continued to burn through the sergeant. "Over there is what I assume you're looking for."

To the left of the open kitchen leading into the patio was a small table centered by an orange and brown trellis. A half-dozen bottles of Tito's private stock lay on their sides, wrapped in chilled, white towels.

Emerging from the kitchen came the peripatetic Teresa, carrying a large wooden platter of peeled fruits. David walked to her, placing a hand on the small of her back.

"Ooh, David, I've never seen you so brash in public."

"Can't help it. You have this strange effect on me."

"I hope it lasts, because we're going to be here for quite some time." Teresa transferred the heavy platter to Angie Perez who, with her sister, carried it over to a picnic table. "And speaking of which," Teresa continued, back peddling toward the kitchen, "it's time I got back to greeting our guests."

David smiled, saluting her with the tip of the spatula.

With the sergeant and priest splintered off toward the wine table, David excused himself, allowing Tito to resume his culinary duties. The teacher spotted a stone bench near a circular row of manicured hedges, and maneuvered toward it. Multiple colors of the pungent flora appeared before him. David closed his eyes, surrendering to the aromatic bouquets of rose, jasmine, violets, and mimosa.

When next he opened them, David flinched, startled by the bespectacled presence of the gauntly looking priest. Backlit by the evening sun, Father Gomez looked eerie, almost ethereal.

"Señor Sherry, I hope I'm not disturbing you. Do you have a moment?"

"Uh, certainly, please have a seat. I was just sitting back admiring our host's beautiful grounds."

The priest nodded. "Yes, magnificent, isn't it? He's

91

very proud of his patio and garden. He has what you Americans call…a brown thumb."

David laughed. "I think you mean a green thumb."

"Oh yes, a green thumb," he repeated self-consciously. "Anyway, I just wanted to reiterate what I said earlier about our community being happy to have you here. We're slow to take to new people in our village, but more and more of us are learning of your good work with the children. I hope you're now seeing a more hospitable side of us."

There was no question about that, David concurred with a shake of his head. Villagers who had shunned him earlier in the school year were now taking measures to approach him. They actively inquired about his health, and even invited him to coffee. Flattered by all this positive attention, David still retained some cynicism, believing it had more to do with his involvement with their beloved Teresa than his skills as an educator.

"Well, as I said, the students are so self-motivated that they make my job very easy."

"Ha, that's what I like about you Norte Americanos. So at ease in deferring praise. We Mexicanos are a bit different. We accept kudos only if we're sure it really isn't from the heart."

Impressed by the priest's wit, David raised his glass. "Then, Father, how about a toast? To modesty."

"Why, what a lovely concept. To modesty." They chinked their empty glasses together and, mockingly, drained them of their spirits. When they'd finished their little ceremony, the priest pressed closer, placing his palm to David's elbow. "We've someone here at the party who also seems quite motivated by your presence, no?"

No explanation was needed. "You too, Padre?" David sighed.

"Just concerned about the welfare of my flock, Señor Sherry." A playful grin spread across his face.

By nine o'clock the house was packed with guests. As was his custom, Tito centered himself among his guests, bellowing out anecdotes in decibels that matched the harmonious tunes of the hired mariachi band. Amid the festivities, no one seemed to notice a huddled couple stealing their way to the far end of the garden.

After considerable effort, David managed to open a rusted wrought iron gate that screeched defiantly. Pulling it aside, the couple was met by a low-arching moon that silhouetted the hilly dunes that led to the sea.

Free from the confines of Tito's grounds, they broke into a run, leaving a trail of clothing in their wake. The naked couple reached the water within a second of one another, both diving headlong into the breakers and bobbing to the surface thirty feet from shore.

David swam up to Teresa only to see her turn toward the open sea, forcing him to give chase. He groaned in frustration, then raced after her with even, powerful strokes. Teresa peered over her right shoulder and shrieked excitedly, seeing how quickly he had cut into her lead. She gave in, breaking off her sprint, and lay back, awaiting the fast approaching David.

"Oh David, enough," Teresa panted, reaching to him for support. "You swim like a fish." She coiled herself around him, recognizing the sensation of David's erection, which she bound tightly to her thighs. They bobbed about the quiet waters, oblivious to an agitated flock of weary gulls watching them from shore. As clouds passed across the moonlit landscape, the tandem worked their way back to the beach, where they made love.

That particular night, however, an additional guardian emerged from beyond the dunes. His concerned stare, magnified and transparent, centered on the nude lovers. He drew back his binoculars and preened a mustache, which curled from the upturned corners of his mouth. A moment later, confident that things were going well between the lovers, Tito Alvarez was gone, returning to his guests.

David and Teresa worked their way back to Tito's home, disheveled but content. They retrieved their clothes, assembled themselves, and sneaked back into the garden, where they sought the attention of their host. Teresa found her uncle and apologized for their temporary disappearance, explaining that both were overcome by the long events of the day and thought a short walk along the beach might revitalize them. With some difficulty, Tito managed to control his inclination to laugh, biting his upper lip and hoping he was conveying to them a look of sincerity. "Yes, I can see you both look...worn out. Why don't you go home? I'll make sure to inform the guests of your situation. I'm sure they'll understand."

He led them to a side exit adjacent to a garden shed which led to the street. When Tito judged them to be out of earshot he burst out in laughter, tears streaming from his eyes. He rejoined the party, stowing his private joke for later reflection.

Spotting Sergeant Arroyo making his way into the house, Tito called to him. He noticed Anna, one of his newly hired girls, standing just inside the glass enclosure to the living room, apparently waiting for the officer. The sergeant looked at the woman, threw up his hands in submission, then turned resignedly to Tito.

"Sí, jefe," said Arroyo.

Tito draped a log of an arm around Arroyo and led him to the garden.

"I only wanted to tell you, Virgilio, that I know you're under a lot of pressure to find Lucy's killer, but I have great confidence in you."

The sergeant straightened, his face registering both relief and confusion over Tito's words. "Thank you very much for your confiden—"

Tito cut him off. "I'm not finished. I also want to remind you that I need to be kept apprised daily of any progress. Is that understood?"

"Oh, sí, jefe, without question."

Tito stepped back, evaluating Arroyo's obsequious posture. Were he hunched any lower, he'd be mistaken for a kowtowing coolie.

"Good," concluded Tito. "Now let's get back to the party. Can I get you something else to drink? Wine? Beer?

A cocktail, perhaps?"

"Frankly, Señor Tito," he said, trembling. "I sure could use something stronger, if you don't mind. Would a double whiskey be out of line?"

Chapter Eight

Officer Muela sat at his desk, barely able to contain himself. He paced nervously about the office, checking the wall clock then confirming it with his watch. His sergeant was forty-five minutes late, no doubt hung over from last night's party. "But just wait until he hears the news," Muela said aloud. He looked down at the notes he'd scribbled.

Only minutes earlier, Muela returned from the toilet after relieving himself of his third cup of coffee when the phone rang. It was the State Headquarters Homicide Bureau. Muela listened intently as a Lieutenant Escobar explained that less than eighteen hours ago, a prostitute had been attacked and killed in neighboring Ascunción. She'd been found by her pimp, nude and mutilated, her upper lip partially removed. The lower lip, faring no better, had been bitten through and literally torn from her face.

The lieutenant went on to say that not only was the M.O. the same, but that the suspect was clearly identified as Ramon Vega. He'd literally run into a policeman as he fled from the whorehouse. As they locked arms, Vega overpowered the officer, pummeling him with near lethal blows to the head, before tossing him to the ground. When he saw that the lawman was in no condition to retaliate, Vega sprinted up the street.

The officer, clearly impaired and reeling from the attack, managed to reach for his pistol. He fired two shots at a distance of about fifty feet, the second bullet striking Vega in the calf. The one-eyed man tumbled forward onto the hard walkway, then picked himself up, dragging his useless leg over a fence before losing himself among the shantytown hutches of Asunción.

In his attempt to follow the suspect, the policeman was overcome by his head injury, losing consciousness within the first few steps of his pursuit. Though Vega escaped, authorities were confident that the wounded murderer would soon be apprehended. All neighboring departments and hospitals were to be notified.

Officer Muela grinned, smacking the paper with the back of his hand. *Sergeant Arroyo, you don't know it yet, but today just might be your lucky day.*

The next few days, however, passed uneventfully. Although there'd been no news of a capture, the village seemed more at ease, sure of Vega's imminent arrest. Besides, they had a new concern: a storm that lay about a day offshore, slowly gathering momentum. By midweek it had joined forces with the late longitudinal winds of spring, moving from the Gulf of Tehuantepec and heading in the general direction of Mancha Negra. According to weather reports, these potentially destructive winds could level an area two hundred miles in diameter.

As a precautionary measure, the fishing villages and farming communities throughout the districts of Oaxaca and Guerrero began battening down their hatches. Sergeant Arroyo sent Muela to David's home to inform him that school would be closed the next day. The young officer then drove back into town, helping merchants board up their windows and secure their wares. As he motored up the street toward San Cristobal, he saw Father Gomez making preparations to help those who planned to take refuge in the church. A line of nearly three dozen people had begun to form from atop the steps.

***

Intrigued by the news, David awoke early the following day and stepped outside, his hands in his pockets. He stared to the north, beyond the village to the inland river. Dozens of men, young and old, raced along the tributary, assisting the fishermen in pulling their boats ashore and anchoring them to the whitewashed trunks of aging palms clustering the estuary.

David gleaned at a tranquil sky, which seemed to belie any cause for alarm. The weather was exceedingly placid, with an occasional cotton ball cloud drifting lazily overhead. David stepped farther out near the edge of the road and examined the sea, hoping to get a better reading of the storm. Squinting, he could see a low riding swatch of ominously dark clouds running parallel to the horizon.

"It's coming," he yelled to non-existent ears. David

looked again at the scurrying humanity below him. Realizing this was not the time for histrionics, he ran from his house and steadily began working his way down the road, his eyes never leaving the sea. Carlos Lopez was the first to see his teacher.

"Hola, Señor Sherry. Over here." Waving his arms above his head, Carlos signaled his teacher forward. All around the American, people such as the Lopez family struggled to beach their skiffs.

David removed his shoes and stepped into the turgid waters. "Thought you boys could use a little help."

"*Gracias, Profesór*, we could. Can you grab the rail near the stern behind me?" David complied, wading deeper into the water while Carlos's father, Jesus, and his uncle positioned themselves on the other side. Together they pushed the skiff forward, aided by the buoyant water until they hit the shallows. Abruptly the hull came to a thudded halt, grounded in the sandy subsurface.

"Now comes the hard part," roared Jesus. "We must get the boat to our shoulders." David followed the movements of the others and bent down in a three-point stance, pressing his shoulders into the crux of bow and stern.

"When I count to three we lift her up and move under the hull, understand?" Although nodding affirmatively, David doubted they could really pull this off. A water logged old hulk like this must weigh hundreds of pounds, he surmised. David looked from one man to the next. Carlos, although not quite seventeen, was small by American standards: no more than five feet four and weighing about one hundred and thirty pounds. His father and uncle, though an inch or two taller, certainly didn't weigh much more.

"Maybe we should get some help," cautioned David.

"Help?" cried the uncle. "Look around you. There is no one to spare."

On all points of the beach, each fisherman was facing the same struggle. Some had moved slightly ahead of others, but none had successfully moored their boats to the trees. Still others were seen churning through the sea, having only recently become aware of the perilous weather conditions.

It took most of the afternoon for the tiny fleet to secure their skiffs. The occasional straggler was met at water's edge by exhausted seamen, weary, but eager to help their brethren of the sea. Winds were beginning to whip up tiny filaments of sand, pelting the men as they retreated to safety.

David followed a line of fishermen who took refuge behind an old sea wall. There they squatted, planting their backs to the leeward side of the massive cement barrier, and waited. Occasionally, one of the fishermen would scoot along the outer edge of the wall to assess the condition of their boats.

The waiting seemed interminable. David's heart raced in anticipation of the impending tempest. He felt reasonably sure, however, of Teresa's safety, estimating the distance from the shoreline to the cantina at approximately half a mile.

Examining the demeanor of the men huddled next to him, David was surprised to see that none seemed to be particularly edgy. Conversations seemed phlegmatic, their posturing almost prankish. Someone passed a pack of cigarettes around, and one by one the fishermen selected a smoke, inhaling them in broad, deep breaths.

Jesus Lopez accurately judged the worried look of his son's teacher. He elbowed Carlos and whispered into his ear. The boy nodded obediently, placed something into his pocket, and crawled over to his mentor. "Señor Sherry, my father says you're not to worry. We're quite used to these storms. Most of them pass quickly." Carlos then drew from his pocket the now crushed Marlboro box, which contained a last cigarette. "Papa says you have earned this. Perhaps it will calm you."

"I'll smoke it a little later if it's okay." He extracted the smoke and held it up in gratitude. But before he had time to react, a sudden gust of wind snatched it, sending the cigarette toppling along the beach, where it disintegrated into a hundred different pieces.

With the winds pressuring the seas forward like some cancerous scourge, onrushing waters began swallowing up large chunks of shoreline. Waves reached the banks of the estuary, lapping over in unbalanced syncopation. David jumped at a hollowed, booming sound given off by a tethered boat that slammed against an anchored palm. A section from the fishtailing bow splintered in half, scattering itself among the trees.

Still, the men appeared relatively unfazed, though their dialog became disjointed and earlier prattle was reduced to mere utterances. Four men running from a dilapidated boat shed caught David's attention. Leaning forward and bent low, they struggled across the sand to a nearby skiff, which had loosened itself from its mooring. One man pounced on the overturned shell, arms stretched to meet the width of the boat, while his partners grabbed the withered hemp and deftly recoiled it around the tree trunk. Invading winds tore at their clothing, while sand blasted away at their eyes. Once secured, the men retreated back to the shed where another fisherman waited, his weight shoved against the opened door, clearing their way to safety.

It didn't take long for David to realize there were several clusters of men sheltered around the beach. Looking beyond the shed, he saw movement near the remains of a keel from an old Canadian steamer. Nearly twenty-five feet of its backbone remained, and several heads could be counted hiding among her rotted, traversing redwood ribs.

Thirty paces from the hulk a brightly colored shirt was spotted wedging itself behind the eroded colonnade of small cliffs leading to the estuary. David stirred with emotion. These proud reapers of the sea, weary mothers keeping an ever vigilant eye on their precious children. How many hundreds of years had this scene been re-enacted? And how much longer would it endure?

The dissonant winds, deafening as they were,

slowly began yielding to the matriculating rains. First they appeared in the guise of softened droplets. David welcomed this cool moisture, which nipped at the accompanying humidity. Feeling noticeably calmer, he sat on the spongy sand, his legs extended in front of him, his sagging shoulders and head supported by the concrete wall. Despite what he was about to undergo, David had little doubt that this is where he wanted to be. He was becoming a viable part of the community, something he was never quite sure he'd accomplished back home. Back home. Strange words to a man who worked in a shunned environment among an alienated group of kids, teaching wholesale rhetoric and dispensing bandages instead of cures. If only there had been a way to reach them. Could he not have extracted just a little more effort from them? From himself?

His attempt at finding an answer to these musings was broken by the vision of a lone man striding across the sand. He appeared to be quite elderly, walking with the aid of a cane. David called out a warning, but the old man, either choosing to ignore him or incapable of hearing him, continued his path toward the sea. With every few steps he'd stop and rotate his head from side to side, then cautiously sniff the air.

Poking half a face around the sea wall, David continued to watch this stranger, completely bewildered by his actions. David turned back to his comrades and realized they also had seen him. "What is that old man —?"

"Shhhh," replied a bearded fisherman, leaning into

David. "Watch."

David cast his eyes back toward the figure, who now stood at the water's edge. He seemed to be examining only those waves strong enough to break through to the estuary. When he'd seen a score of such waves, he reversed himself, facing the men from behind the sea wall. He nodded slightly, tapped his limping leg with the cane, and then tossed the supporting stick headlong into the sand.

From their numerous lees of protection the fishermen emerged, walking tentatively at first before breaking into a mad dash toward the old man.

David stared in disbelief. What were they doing? He shifted in the direction of the moored skiffs laying listlessly in banks of sand. As he inched himself up along the wall, David felt a sharp tap on his shoulder. He turned, thinking it was the bearded fisherman, but instead found a blown piece of driftwood nestled against his arm. It was then that he discovered he was alone; the others had filed out along the other end of the barricade and joined forces with five or six additional squads of men, each laughing and shaking hands with the enigmatic old man.

Carlos stood with the men for a moment then withdrew, taking a step in David's direction. Raising his hands to his mouth, he shouted. "Señor Sherry, come out. It's safe."

The shaken teacher, not completely comforted by Carlos's words, called back, "What happened?"

"Alfonso has told us the storm has broken." Pointing to the white-haired man, Carlos moved even closer to

David, oblivious to the cry of a circling tern. "Alfonso is our village shaman. He carries the gift of prediction. Look at him, maestro. He has dropped his cane. His limp is gone."

The two stood facing each other. "I never knew you had a shaman in your village."

"Oh yes, señor. He lives in a small hut near the far end of the fork, but he is seldom seen during the day. Mostly, he walks about at night searching the skies for problems."

"And you believe this man?" David queried.

"*Como no?* Alfonso knows more about the impending evils of nature here in Mancha Negra than anyone I've ever seen. Maybe it's because he's seen many things in his hundred years of life. But whatever the case, as you can see, the storm has broken."

David scratched his head and scanned the expanse of sea and sky. Indeed, the storm appeared to be in a deliquescing mood. Chunks of sky, darkened moments before by ominous clouds, now began blossoming into hues of silver and blue.

Shortly after, the arduous process of returning the boats to the water began. The fishermen toiled with neither expression nor hint of discord. There was work to be done and mouths to feed. In fact, David sensed rejuvenation in their labors. Among the myriad pieces of driftwood and kelp lying about at every turn, the men continued on, doggedly re-entering their ocean mistress and her awaiting harvest.

David followed Carlos back to his father and uncle,

who'd already unleashed their skiff and sat patiently waiting for them. Lifting the boat in unison, they traipsed back into the water, their ankles enveloped by the viscous, black soup of storm debris. The cold currents effused by the storm cooled their initial efforts, startling David.

"Brrr," he complained, his limbs breaking out in goosebumps.

"Just a little farther," he heard one of the men urge. David's teeth chattered in affirmation as he signaled his understanding.

They placed the skiff roughly into the mouth of the estuary. Carlos's uncle hefted himself aboard and grasped his makeshift mainsail. He unfurled it, ramming it into the holder plate, and slid the boom through the sheet. Carlos motioned for David to move aft, where together they could propel the boat into deeper water.

They'd taken it to about four feet of water when Jesus cried, "Let go. The winds are catching her." At the last second, Carlos's uncle was pulled aboard and made his way to the tiller. David gladly released the skiff, hearing the whoosh of the wind-filled canvas, but his own inertia pulled him forward. By the time the boat was underway, David was neck-deep in water, ineptly dodging a series of wakes that nearly toppled him.

Carlos and David back peddled, watching the two fishermen as they guided their skiff to open sea, their sail at a right angle, running with the wind. The American was nearing the point of exhaustion, and readily accepted Carlos's guiding support back to shore. Unable to lift his legs against the resistance of the water, David shuffled forward in small steps, his arm draped around the young man's shoulder.

"There's no way on earth I'd have made it as a fisherman," he panted. "Obviously, there's more to it than just casting nets and hauling in your catch."

The boy's teeth gleamed. "Sí, Señor Sherry, it is not so easy. But it is a healthy life, no?"

"Sure, if you're Charles Atlas. My back is killing me." David released himself from Carlos, rotating his shoulder in windmill fashion. "Ah, to be your age again, Carlo—"

"Maestro!" Though spoken by the young man at a level of unassuming calm, the word held with it the betrayal of distress. David stared at him in uncertainty.

"Carlos?"

"Devilfish! Aieeeh!" Carlos stared down at the waters directly beneath him, and raised his left foot just above the surface. Revealing itself was an obscurely colored sea creature about ten inches in length. Its massive head and bulbous eyes followed Carlos's retreat. Red-ringed gills opened and closed, revealing a column of two inch needle-like growths running along its dorsal fin. Indignantly, it moved even closer to the exposed second foot, then halted, apparently content with the damage it had inflicted. Reversing itself, the fish turned away from Carlos, zigzagging its way into open water at a leisurely pace.

The stinger had entered the heel of the boy's foot, but had broken in half as Carlos pulled away. "Señor Sherry, *por favor.*"

David lifted the leg of the injured foot and dragged him the remaining few feet to shore.

Carlos spoke pleadingly to his mentor. "You must remove it. You must...." He grimaced in pain, grabbing David's shirt and squeezing tightly. A quick survey of the wound showed only a slight trickling of blood oozing from the puncture, but the foot was already beginning to swell. Without hesitation, David held the boy tightly about the waist then reached down and plucked the barb out, removing a thumb nail length of spine. Carlos howled uncontrollably, then turned flush. David eased him down onto the sand, using one hand to dig a small mound on which to elevate his head.

His breathing labored, Carlos indicated that he was feeling a little better, but David remained unconvinced. Unsure of what to do next, he looked around for help and was relieved to see two men approaching, one behind the other. The one in front was Omar Velasquez, the slow witted church groundskeeper. He appeared to be no older than Carlos.

"Carlos, what's wrong?" he questioned, assessing his friend through thickly lensed glasses.

David answered in his stead, pointing at the poisonous spine laying in the sand. "Please, go get a doctor."

"There is no doctor in Mancha Negra," he said simply.

"Then, can you find Teresa Santos?"

Omar thought for a moment, then smiled. "I know Teresa, she's a friend of mine. Would you like me to get her?"

Keeping his exasperation in check, David sighed deeply, then repeated his instructions. Omar nodded, blinking a couple of times as if to clear his head, then turned on his heels, making tracks toward the Club El Gato.

"May I see the foot?"

David had forgotten about the second man. He looked up to see the bent figure of the old shaman. His tanned face contrasted with his wispy white mane. But it was the penetrating clarity of his blue eyes that caught David's attention.

"My name is Alfonso," he said, his eyes squarely riveted on the boy's foot. He thrust out an arthritic index finger, which he ran gingerly over the wound. Carlos heaved, extending his quivering leg. "Devilfish," Alfonso said definitively.

"That's what Carlos said as well." David reached for the stinger, handing it to the shaman.

Alfonso stroked his blanched goatee. "This kind of fish usually doesn't stray this close to shore. The storm must have brought it in."

Feeling his knees beginning to cramp, David shifted his weight. He looked woefully at Carlos, whose eyes appeared nearly closed. "Is he going to be all right?"

"Well, it's a good thing the spine caught him on the heel. It doesn't look like it penetrated too deeply. Luck is with him today. Had this devilfish planted one of his spines a little closer to the arch...." Alfonso's voice trailed off, leaving David to interpret his meaning. "A fisherman from Dos Cruces was struck there about fifteen years ago. He was dead within an hour."

The shaman stood up, taking with him a handful of bloodstained sand, which he threw near the spot where Carlos was stung. "The best you can do is get him home right away. If you wait a moment, I'll get my grandson, Aldo, to help you."

He called feebly at someone laying out netting near the old shed. Aldo looked up, shading his eyes. Sensing trouble, he dropped his fishing gear and began a sprint toward his grandfather.

David returned his concentration to Carlos. The foot, now pulpy and discolored, had swelled to grotesque proportions. A corpulent ankle protruded beyond the bridge of the foot, swaddling the toes within its fleshy overlay.

The boy's eyes opened suddenly and his head jerked upwards, nearly hitting David's.

"Oh God, oh God, the pain!" he screamed. David cradled Carlos's head in his hands, and at once felt the student's vomit spew into his lap. The purging, however, eased the discomfort of his violent spasms, and left his breathing noticeably less strained.

David hardly had time to react to the boy's convulsions when he heard the laborious movements of feet trudging in the sand behind him. Then he remembered the shaman's grandson.

"Thank God. Quickly, let's get him up." The two men

111

lifted the limp body, with Aldo grabbing the head and shoulders, while David controlled the boy's legs. They'd gone no more than twenty yards when David heard the unmistakable voice of Teresa.

Running along the narrow frontage road that paralleled the estuary, she leaped into the sand and hurdled a small set of dunes, which led her to the three men. "Put him down, but carefully. I want to see the foot." The two bearers did as she commanded, gently placing Carlos on a drying patch of sand. Teresa circled Carlos, first checking his pupils, then casting a disquieting conspectus at the wound.

"Carlos, can you hear me?" Her voice was typically clear and soothing. "This is Teresa. You're going to be fine." She waited a few seconds, looking for some sort of reaction. But his only movement was a barely discernable rise and fall of his chest.

Teresa knelt down, grabbed an icy hand, and repeated his name. "Carlos…. Carlos…," she called out, this time cupping both hands around his left ear like a megaphone and mouthing his name between her thumbs.

When again he failed to respond, the fisherman commented, "He's done for."

"Shut up," screamed an angry Teresa. "Quickly, get him back up and we'll take him to my house."

***

Carlos slept most of that day under the vigilant care of Teresa, his condition fluctuating between comatose and semi-consciousness. She thoroughly cleansed his wound with a wet vinegar compress, changing it in two hour intervals. To control the swelling, Teresa wrapped ice chips around a second compress, which extended from foot to mid-calf.

Bone weary, the young prostitute plunked herself down in her old wicker chair and drew her hands to her face, rubbing them tightly against her skin. Despite her fatigue, Teresa was keenly aware of others in the room, most notably Carlos's family, who had assembled on a couch facing the young man. Azucena, Carlos's teary eyed mother, sat at one end of the couch, her tiny hands wringing a tattered tissue.

The late-arriving Father Gomez entered the room, stopping first to enquire about Carlos before attending to the grieving family. He went down the line, offering words of spiritual comfort to each member, understandably sympathetic to their stunned lethargy. As he approached Azucena, the woman leaped from the couch, falling on her knees and pulling at the hand of the clergyman.

"Please, Padre, don't let God take my Carlos. Not now, not now. He's my baby."

Father Gomez took hold of her wrist, pulling her up to him. "There, there Azucena. Carlos couldn't be in better hands. The best thing we can do right now is to pray for the courage to hold fast at a time like this. You do want to be strong now, don't you? Of course you do." He moved his hand to her cheek, pressing it warmly, then suggested they pray together in silence.

Tito Alvarez stood nearby, his Panama held modestly

at his side, his broad back leaning against an old dresser. He'd overheard the priest's words, and fought hard not to cynically ask in whose hands he had meant: Teresa's or God's. The pimp then shifted his attention to across the room, where his niece still sat, hunched in a chair. Teresa's eyes appeared closed, oblivious to the man standing beside her. His hand touched Teresa's shoulder, jarring her from her stupor.

"Teresa, honey, one cup of coffee as requested." The Mexicana looked up somberly at David. "I told the bartender you wanted it strong," he said. David's mouth puckered in mock disgust at the dense, black liquid in the cup. "Looks like motor oil to me."

"Thank you, David." She gulped fully, awaiting the effects of the caffeine. David draped an arm over her shoulder.

"How's he doing?"

"I don't know," she sighed. "He really should have awakened by now."

"Is there anything I can do?"

Teresa managed a perfunctory smile and patted David's hand. "Well, since you asked. You can remove that ice pack from his ankle. It needs replenishing. I'd do it myself, but frankly, I don't think I have the strength to get off this chair right now."

David stepped to the end of the bed, where he began the procedure. He lifted the ankle and began unwrapping the compress that held the flaccid ice bag. A slight tug at a knot produced an angry protestation from Carlos. "Ow,

114

go easy with that, maestro."

The room sprang to life and everyone surged forward, surrounding the bed. Señora Lopez, the first to reach him, grabbed her son's hand, kissing it repeatedly. Her unkempt boy, his eyes darkly circled, smiled thinly. Carlos looked about the room, acknowledging each well-wisher with a slight nod or wink.

Tito was the last to come forward, appearing as haggard as the boy. The pimp had always been fond of Carlos. He recalled the enterprising youngster spending weekend afternoons camped outside the Club El Gato with a small shoeshine box, picking up pesos from the local men bent on impressing the girls inside.

"You're looking good, boy," he said, his eyes purposely averting the wound. "Soon you'll be on your feet and back in the classroom, eh, Señor Sherry?"

"Absolutely. He's not getting out of his exams so easily." A chorus of laughter surrounding Carlos broke the tension in the room.

"Now, everybody," declared Teresa, "I think it's time we gave this boy some quiet time." She surveyed Señora Lopez, who bobbed her head in agreement.

"Bless you, Teresa, for all you've done for my boy." Azucena rose with the help of her husband and joined the exiting crowd. They left the room, one by one, leaving only David, who hung back to assist Teresa.

As soon as everyone had left, David went to the door, locking it. "You could use some rest yourself. Why don't you grab a couple of hours sleep and I'll watch Carlos."

Yielding to a yawn, Teresa rose to her feet. She clasped her hands above her head and began the twisting and stretching routine that David had found so excitable once before.

"No, I'm fine," she remarked. "Gloria will relieve me in a little while when she gets off work. You should go home and prepare for your class tomorrow. I'll join you as soon as I can."

Teresa quietly edged up to David, moving her mouth to within an inch of his ear. "I could use a kiss before you go, however."

David shot her his crooked smile. He fondled her neck and delivered a lengthy kiss. "Try not to be too late," he reminded her, placing Teresa's hand on his thigh.

CHAPTER NINE

Friday morning portended to be a scorcher. The omnipresent westerly breezes, normally a reliable cooling source, were replaced by a general malaise, giving rise to the garrulous sounds of buzzing cicadas and palm flies that stirred the air in a ceaseless drone.

David arrived at school looking as though he'd run a marathon in his work clothes.

He ripped at his tie, stuffing it in his breast pocket, and thrust a handful of fingers through the matted hair glued to his skull. Even his youthful students, normally impervious to this kind of heat, moved uncomfortably in their seats, sliding their chairs near the partially repaired windows in the hope of catching a hint of a breeze. Getting through this day was going to be tough. The entire class had begun preparing for their final three weeks of exams, spending the first part of the day broken up into discussion groups and drilling one another from hundreds of pages of copious notes.

Hour after hour they sat, fiercely debating over sentence structure and syntax, while David moved among them acting as facilitator. He had little to do and felt somewhat impotent and uncreative, so self-directed were these young people. Still, David marveled at the focus of this close-knit group, thinking how the absence of Carlos must be affecting them. Here they were, twelve anxious and undaunted students who, while engrossed over their studies, would steal an occasional look at the empty desk in the front row.

As the day drew to an end, David offered a suggestion. "I know how concerned you are about your classmate, and I'm sure he'd like to see you. Yesterday evening Carlos woke and seemed in good spirits." The news invoked a rousing cheer from the students. "I'm going to check on him in about an hour and a half. If you would like to meet me at Teresa's at about 4:30, we can surprise him."

The entire group eagerly agreed; at precisely the designated hour David saw the congregation of students milling outside Teresa's door just as he was approaching her home. He waved to them approvingly and walked to the front door, knocking twice. Teresa answered, opening the door only slightly. She appeared edgy as she gazed at the assembled group outside. This, David construed, was a bad omen.

Sarita Sanchez, an auburn-haired girl with wire-rimmed glasses, stepped forward. "Teresa, the class and I were wondering how Carlos is getting along."

"Shhh," warned Teresa. "He's napping right now." She eased the door shut behind her and addressed the students. "Carlos is still pretty weak, but he is recovering.

I'd rather he not have any company right now. When he awakens I'll be sure to tell him of your visit. It should really cheer him up."

"Then how about tomorrow?" asked the persevering student.

"We'll see. I'll let Señor Sherry know if there's any improvement. Now I've got to get back inside. Go on now."

Reluctantly the students began their slow walk home. David stepped up onto the crumbling porch and took Teresa's elbow, hustling her back into her quarters. He noted she had spoken to the students without even a hint of a smile, something uncharacteristic for the normally amicable Teresa.

"So, how is Carlos, really?"

Teresa brought a finger to David's lips. "Right now his fever's down and he's alert," she said, sotto voce. "But, there is still major swelling. We've kept ice on it all night, but the infection appears to be moving up the leg. If it doesn't go down by morning, I've got to get him to the clinic at Maldonaldo. It's only fourteen kilometers southeast of here. I'd prefer to take him to Acapulco, but it's just too far, and much of the road north of here is filled with ruts."

"Can you get someone to go with you?"

"Uncle Tito will go with me, and he'll probably bring Maximilian and another one of his men. We shouldn't have any trouble."

David ran a hand over the back of his neck. "Maybe…

119

maybe I should go with you. I could cancel my — "

"No, absolutely not. It is much more important that you stay here and prepare your students for their exams. They're counting on you."

"Yeah," said David. "I guess you're right. But perhaps I can get hold of Lopez's Jeep tomorrow after work and drive over to the hospital. Do you think you'll be there for a while?"

"Most likely. But we're getting ahead of ourselves. Let's wait and see how he is tomorrow. It's quite possible he could recover on his own."

***

It took but a cursory look at the bulged wrapping for Teresa to make her decision. Even without touching the leg the heat of infection radiated from the ugly mass. She went to the phone and notified her uncle.

They reached the clinic in Maldonaldo in less than an hour. It was situated just east of town, and consisted of two World War II Quonset huts placed end to end. The grounds were fashioned after a Japanese-style gravel garden, and were bordered by freshly painted white boulders.

Teresa was well acquainted with the clinic, having done some volunteering there prior to her days as a nursing student. The first building contained an admitting office and hospital ward, while the second housed an examination room and a small but well-stocked surgery, capable of handling intermediate emergencies.

Tito's big Chrysler fishtailed to a stop near the emergency entrance, coughing and sputtering, even as

Teresa, Tito, and Carlos moved well away from the car. Rumbling up the road behind them in a Chevy pickup came Maximilian. He intercepted his boss and Teresa, lifting the boy into his arms with minimal effort. Teresa ran ahead of them, holding open the wide double doored portals.

A blast of cool air from a portable air conditioner mounted in the corner hit each of them as they passed through the door. "Ah," moaned Tito, using stubby fingers to wipe the grit from under his neck. "This is much better." He glanced about the room, getting his bearings. Directly in front of him sat a woman behind a small mahogany desk. Placed around the desk were five metal fold-out chairs, the nearest one precariously accepting the overweight pimp.

"Can I help you?" The woman's voice was young, girlish, far different from her appearance.

Tito flinched, uneasy with this odd contrast. He guessed her to be in her late thirties, with short wavy hair and glasses listing at the end of her nose. As she stood up Tito viewed her hospital dress, which he surmised was three sizes too large and overtly prudish. Never comfortable with this type of woman, he turned helplessly to his niece.

"Yes," said Teresa. "We've brought in a very sick boy from our village."

"Stepped on a devilfish." blurted Tito. "He's — "

"Just a minute," the admitting clerk declared. She glanced quickly at Carlos, who still remained in

121

Maximilian's arms, and then reached for a clipboard that hung on the wall behind her. Facing Tito, she began her line of questioning.

"The name of the sick or injured person?"

"Carlos Lopez."

"Age?"

"Age? Oh, I'm not sure. Teresa?"

"Sixteen," she interjected.

"Address?"

Tito felt himself fidgeting in his seat. "Um...I don't know. Look, if you can just have someone look at him. He's—"

"Our nurse is with someone right now and will probably be unavailable for at least another ten minutes, so let's get this information out of the way. This won't take much longer."

Tito slumped deeper into his chair, expelling a long submissive breath. He removed his hat and traced a finger over the black silk strip surrounding the crown. "All right, señora, what information would you like?"

Teresa, meanwhile, helped Maximilian lower Carlos into a chair. He was having difficulty with his vision, and in a slurred voice called out her name. "I'm right here," she said, brushing back his hair from his forehead.

Completely absorbed with Carlos's welfare, Teresa was unaware of the silent swishing of drapery unfolding behind her. Nurse Juanita Calderon entered, her hands widened above her head as she pushed apart the canvas curtain. She wore a powder blue sweater over a heavily starched white dress. Her legs were draped in white stockings that contrasted with her plain black leather shoes. Calderon's eyes, set slightly above a bobbed, porcine-shaped nose, were heavily made up to accentuate their bluish-grey cast. Wisps of curly blonde hair extended beyond her cap.

Nurse Calderon presented a formal smile to the forlorn quartet, then looked questioningly at the admitting clerk, who handed her the chart. As she perused Carlos's medical history, Tito withdrew from the chair. He flicked imaginary debris from his trousers and introduced himself, thinking perhaps his modest reputation might speed things along.

The nurse looked up at him momentarily, giving Tito her most unimpressed look, then shifted her attention back to the chart. Once finished, she moved to Carlos and inspected his foot. "Someone's done an excellent job of treating this wound."

"My niece," Tito exclaimed. "She was studying to be a nurse."

"Please, Uncle," pleaded a red faced Teresa.

The nurse continued with her examination. "There is some infection and discoloring, but with the proper antibiotics he should fully recover. We will need to keep him here for a few days of observation."

Forcing a hard swallow, Tito spoke up. "No offense, señora. I'm sure you've correctly diagnosed this thing, but I'd like a doctor's opinion on this, as well."

"I understand perfectly, Señor Alvarez. However,

he's in surgery right now and, immediately afterwards, has what appears to be a difficult delivery awaiting him at the Altamirano clinic. We have a second doctor on call, and he should be here by early this afternoon."

"Fine then, it's settled." Tito slapped his thigh, his concerns greatly diminished. "We'll keep him here in your care. In the meantime, is there anything else we can do?"

"As a matter of fact, there is. You can help me get this young man into a bed."

Tito agreed and signaled forth Maximilian. The giant reached down, lifting Carlos back into him arms, and followed the nurse and the others through the open drapes to another section of the clinic. The room appeared eerily dark and smelled strongly of disinfectant. The raging air conditioner had little effect on this half of the Quonset hut, as the room temperature was markedly warmer than the waiting room.

On one side of the room, arranged perpendicular to the wall, was a row of six cots, approximately two and one-half feet apart from one another. Three of them were unoccupied. Crisp, clean sheets and wool blankets covered each bed. Opposite the bedding on the other side of the room stood an equal number of small dressers. A large stainless steel medicine cabinet with glass enclosures was secured at the far end of the quarters.

With the first, third, and sixth beds occupied, Nurse Calderon had Maximilian place Carlos on the second cot, between an elderly man lying in a traction belt and a small child with a heavily bandaged left eye and forehead.

124

Neither patient seemed to take notice of the new arrival. The man snored hollowly through a flat, bulbous nose, while the young girl appeared occupied with a large stuffed animal that looked to be on its last legs. A third patient lay on the far bunk closest to the medicine cabinet.

Tito peered at him briefly as he lay on his side, his back to them. The man's head was completely devoid of hair, exposing two tiny elf-like ears. Despite the oppressive heat in the room he appeared chilled, struggling to keep his blanket pulled up tightly about his neck. Left visible, however, was a heavily bandaged leg, coated in a yellowish, antiseptic paint.

"What happened to him?" asked Tito.

Nurse Calderon ignored the question, concentrating on the reading of a thermometer she'd just extracted from Carlos's mouth. "Good, less than three degrees above normal." She shook down the thermometer, then looked up at Tito. "Now, what was your question?"

"That poor man," he said, tossing a thumb in the direction of the bald patient. "He looks very sick."

"He was admitted here yesterday, during the afternoon shift, I think. His chart showed something about a machinery accident." After offering this explanation, Calderon produced a blood pressure cuff, wrapping it snuggly around Carlos's arm. As the pressure tightened, he grimaced slightly. Immediately she deflated the cup, grinning at the supine youth. "Blood pressure's normal."

"When do you plan to treat his pain?" Teresa inquired.

"I'll leave a message with Dr. Zacaro the moment he

gets out of surgery, requesting Meperdine. He should okay the request without any problem."

As she rose to go Tito stepped forward, adjusting the Panama to his head. "Take good care of him."

"Don't worry, we will." She turned her back to Tito and barked out something to the admitting clerk.

Teresa and her uncle used that moment to gather near Carlos a final time. Despite his immense pain, the young student's countenance displayed a look of alertness that had not been seen since before the incident.

"I'll tell your mother and father of your condition," said Teresa. "I'm sure they'll both want to come up and see you first thing tomorrow morning. That is if the nurse permits it."

"Oh, of course. I won't be here, but I'll inform Nurse Rayonez. She's one of our weekend shift nurses during the day."

A much more confident Tito and his little entourage followed the nurse back through the curtains and into the reception room. They were greeted by an abnormally rotund pregnant woman of eighteen, who was trying her best to squeeze herself between the arm rests of one of the chairs.

"I can see you're very busy," Tito acknowledged, "so we won't keep you any longer. Thank you again."

Nurse Calderon waved off the remarks, already focused on the new patient.

They walked steadily to their cars, undeterred by the intermittent rains they'd been encountering all day.

Maximilian had gotten into his truck and, with a waving hand, motored out of the driveway, heading for the cantina. Teresa and Tito, only now beginning to feel a release from the enormous pressure of the past couple of days, melted back into the sunken leather seats of the old Imperial. After a full minute of silence, Tito cranked over the powerful engine, while Teresa checked her watch, realizing she was in for a very long day.

"Are you ready, my dear?" he asked.

"Yes, let's get back. I'm…oh, damn." A faint look of disgust marked her face. "I've forgotten my shawl. I think I left it hanging on the chair next to Carlos." She reached for the door.

"Teresa, wait here. I'll get it. You've done enough for one day."

Leaving the car idling, Tito dashed back to the clinic. The pregnant girl and Nurse Calderon were positioned exactly as he'd last seen them, although it appeared to Tito that the girl was about to give birth at any moment.

"Yes?" questioned the nurse after seeing the pimp.

"Sorry to interrupt. My niece left her shawl in the ward. May I fetch it?"

The admitting clerk, overhearing the conversation, stood up from her desk. "Señor Alverez, I'll get it for you."

Tito waved her off. "It'll only take a second. Don't bother yourself."

He sped forward, drawing open the curtains and disappearing into the ward. Immediately he spotted the shawl hanging over the chair, and crept silently forward to retrieve it. Tito peeked a look at Carlos, who appeared to be in the throes of a deep sleep, as did his two neighboring companions. As he turned to leave Tito shot a final glance at the patient in the far cot. He was no longer lying down, but had managed to sit himself upright, rotating his body to where he was facing Tito.

His shaved bald head was drooped, apparently assessing his leg wound. He gingerly tapped at the coagulating ooze extending from the bandage. Surprised at its sensitivity, he swore aloud.

Tito tossed the shawl over a shoulder and stared empathetically at the agonizing figure. "Would you like me to get the nurse?"

"What?" The man's head lurched upward, surprised by the presence of the pimp. He stared wildly at Tito, then slowly his eyes narrowed, a contrast of penetrating darkness and fathomless glaze.

Now that the blanket no longer encumbered the patient, Tito felt him strangely familiar. A muscular body propped up by Herculean legs rose to its feet. There was no longer a doubt as to its identity.

"Vega," hissed Tito. The old pimp's rage was immediate, his judgment diluted by the unbridled enmity he'd been carrying since the death of Lucy. "You're going to die, you bastard." Tito ran toward the wobbling killer, but Vega held his ground and, upon watching the aging movements of the pimp, broke out in a sardonic grin. With arms extended, Tito bore into the man, wrapping them around the challenger's waist like some enormous python. Vega retaliated, driving the palm of his hand under Tito's chin and practically lifting the pimp off the ground. But Tito persisted, tenaciously clinging to Vega, his hands locked around the man's waist.

The men held that stance for what seemed an eternity, until Tito, his arms rubbery with exhaustion, began to loosen his grip. Vega jerked back and forth in a twisting motion, hoping that this jostling would further undo Tito's grasp. But his thrashing about resulted in the pimp's knee or foot brushing against Vega's bandaged leg, breaking his concentration and forfeiting whatever strength the one-eyed man had been able to muster.

As a last resort, Vega began to flail at Tito's eyes, but that maneuver was short lived. The strength in his fingers had drained, and he was forced to resort to a dabbing action. It became clear to the pimp that Vega had nothing left with which to continue.

Tito followed the movement of Vega's good eye and watched his fading pupil arc upward, practically blanketed by the whites of his eye. But the visage was calm, almost content, the direction of his stare never deviating and fixed solely beyond Tito. Confusion gave way to trepidation as Tito witnessed a hardened, sinewy jawline transform into an icy, vulturous smile.

"What the—?" uttered Tito aloud, his voice winded and shaken. The grinning expression was the last thing he remembered. That and a bizarre tympanic eruption that flooded his waning thoughts just prior to slipping into a black, liquid abyss.

129

***

Sergeant Arroyo rechecked the restraints before giving the nod to Officer Muela to escort the admitting clerk to the patrol car. "I'll be there in a moment." Pushing apart the blinds from the admissions room window, his eyes followed them through the darkness as they approached the Jeep. The two crossed in front of the high beam headlamps that illuminated the rain in a surreal cast.

Swinging back toward the ward, Arroyo found Nurse Calderon attending to a reclining Teresa, whose left cheek revealed streaks of fingernail marks that ran diagonally from the corner of one eye to her chin. Next to her, teetering against the side of one of the cots, stood Tito, his head tilted back to better balance a large ice pack he'd been holding to the side of his neck.

Arroyo neared Teresa first. She stared back at him passively, not wanting to interfere with the nurse's treatment of her face.

"Looks like nothing more than a good-sized scratch, Teresa," said the sergeant.

She laughed. "Liar—more like a good-sized scar. I guess no more beauty contests for me, huh, Virgilio?"

The sergeant chuckled. "I have a feeling Señor Sherry won't even notice." He bent at the waist and squeezed her shoulder, but his eyes followed the rapidly slumping pimp, who appeared to be more seriously hurt than he initially let on. Arroyo stepped behind Teresa and cautiously placed a supportive hand to the back of Tito, who offered little resistance. It was apparent he was in considerable pain.

"How are you, jefe?"

Tito removed the ice pack and massaged the back of his neck with his hand. "I still don't fully understand why the clerk attacked me with that damned chair." He pointed angrily to the gnarled fold-out chair that lay half-exposed under one of the hospital cots.

"It seems, Señor Alvarez, that our esteemed clerk, Carlotta Rojas, is Vega's sister-in-law." A stunned Tito ceased working his neck and did his best to right himself. "We've been able to establish that while on the run and with his wounds not healing properly, Vega contacted his brother and had him convince his wife to slip him into the clinic between shift changes sometime yesterday afternoon. She filled out a chart listing him as a Señor Quesada, a mechanic from Hornitos who was suffering from a work-related laceration. The timing couldn't have been more perfect. It had been the last day of work for the day shift nurse, Señorita...." Sergeant Arroyo removed a note pad from his back pocket. "Señorita Chavez. She had accepted a new position at a hospital in Acapulco. This made it easy for Señora Rojas. The moment nurse Chavez left, Vega was smuggled in, and she listed Chavez as the primary examination nurse.

"My guess is he intended to stay until Monday morning, then take off before the doctor, whose name she also forged, arrived. With only one ward nurse per shift who is responsible for all departments of the clinic, our admitting clerk had plenty of opportunity to attend to his wounds and disguise his features, such as shaving his

131

head."

Tito searched for a chair, still disbelieving what he was hearing. "Yet he escaped again?" he asked.

"Si, jefe, I'm afraid so." Arroyo pumped a thumb over his shoulder, aiming it at Teresa. "And that's when your niece had that unfortunate accident. Nurse Calderon heard the commotion, saw you and Vega wrestling around, and unknowingly asked the clerk to call the police while she ran out to get Teresa. But when they returned both women saw Señora Rojas leading Vega through the curtain entrance. All four people literally ran into one another. Vega pushed the nurse aside while the clerk tried to screen off Teresa, who was trying to get at Vega. That Rojas is a pretty strong woman. She got hold of Teresa's hair, pulled it toward her, and ripped at her face. You can see the results."

A sickened look from Tito, viewing Teresa's face, attested to Arroyo's remarks. "Sergeant, I heard the clerk's voice a few moments ago. Is she still here?"

"She was. Officer Muela is taking her back to Mancha Negra, where she'll be charged with aiding a fugitive. After she's processed, the federal police will pick her up and take her to Oaxaca."

Tito shifted the contents of the ice bag to another part of his neck. "It's strange that she didn't leave with him."

The sergeant threw up his hands. "Who knows what went through her mind? Nurse Calderon told me that once Vega escaped, Señora Rojas returned to the clinic, headed directly to her desk, and sat, staring calmly at

Nurse Calderon, who at that time was phoning our office for assistance."

Picturing the situation as described by the sergeant, Tito felt vaguely sympathetic. He'd held the value of family in high regard, and could see the clerk's perverted justification for her actions, even though he couldn't condone them. "Blood's thicker than water, eh?" Tito questioned.

"Something like that," answered Arroyo. "The señora told me she's been married to Vega's brother for over twenty years, although she uses her maiden name here at the clinic. Her husband and Vega have remained very close, from what I understand."

The irony of this last revelation left Tito shaking his head in bewilderment. Local tragedies that extended beyond his control had always gnawed at him, rendering him temporarily uneasy. He felt a binding, spastic tug of sphincter muscle.

"Dammit," Tito said. "I've got to relieve myself. Help me up, will you?" Arroyo took Tito's hand and guided him to the far end of the ward where, behind a Plexiglas wall, the toilet was located. The short walk had dwindled the pimp's energy, but he insisted on handling his ablutions by himself.

The sergeant leaned patiently against the other side of the stall, his legs crossed, a hand patting the crest of his rogue wave hairdo. For some reason Arroyo's mood had lightened considerably since today's episode with Vega, possibly because he now knew the killer was more vulnerable than Arroyo had realized. This reverie was cut short, however, by the muffled grunts from the other side of the partition.

"At least, Sergeant, we know he can't get far this time, not with that leg of his."

Arroyo's lips tightened and he uncrossed his legs, pushing himself away from the stall. "Er…. Well, it seems that's not quite correct, jefe. Vega made his escape by stealing a car.

"A car?" roared the returning voice.

"Sí, Señor Alvarez. Um…your car."

Chapter Ten

The return of Carlos to Mancha Negra was reminiscent of a hero's welcome. Most fishermen from the village took a small break from their toils, setting aside their nets for part of that morning to welcome back one of their own. As he passed through the streets, seated proudly in the sergeant's opened patrol Jeep, dozens of townspeople ran alongside, wishing him well and chiding him good naturedly.

"Look, Carlos," yelled his father, seated next to him. "Over by the church."

The boy shaded his eyes and stared in that direction, breaking into a wide smile. Standing on the first tier of the old church steps was David and the entire class. The sergeant approached them and pulled to a stop, allowing Carlos to step out.

"Good to see you up and around," said David, greeting him with a hug. "Are you ready to get back to your books? We've got a lot of hard work ahead of us. Playtime's over."

"Sí, Profesor. Compared to what I went through, studying for exams will seem like...like a walk on the

135

beach."

A student, overhearing his schoolmate's remarks, added glumly, "Sure, providing you look where you step."

The simpering Carlos nodded excitedly in agreement. "Chico, for once you are most certainly right."

The American stood back, allowing Carlos a few minutes to accept the well wishes of his friends. He climbed to the next tier of steps, and then shouted down to his students. "Okay everybody, you heard this young man. He said these exams are going to be a walk on the beach. Let's head back to class and see if he knows what he's talking about."

A shout went up, and two of the teacher's huskier boys raised Carlos to their shoulders and began following David and the others back up the hill toward the schoolhouse. The thirty or so villagers that remained offered Carlos a final salutation before returning to their shops and boats.

***

David sat numbly at his desk, exhausted after an inordinately intense day of instruction. The afternoon lighting had long since abandoned him, leaving David alone within the dusky confines of the ramshackle building. Bussu palms, whose leaves rustled against one side of the school, signaled the commencement of the evening offshore breezes.

David looked at the wall clock behind him. It read 6:10, which in reality meant closer to 6:30. "Shit," he murmured under his breath, remembering his date to meet Teresa at Zia's Restaurant for dinner. Already fifteen minutes late, David randomly grabbed a stack of uncorrected papers from his desk, pinched them together with a paper clip, and threw them into his briefcase. He adjusted his collar then charged out of the room, his mind swirling with outrageous excuses he hoped Teresa would find acceptable.

Zia's, one of only two restaurants in Mancha Negra, was located on the opposite end of the street from the Club El Gato. The building also doubled as a family dwelling, run by the widow, Zia Chacon, a firebrand of a woman whose language was known to be as zesty as her sauces. Teresa sat with her back to the entrance, engaged in small talk with Señora Chacon and another customer. She was unaware of the harried American who blew in from around the corner, his hair flayed at the sides, a paisley tie flung over his shoulder. Breathing hard, David stumbled forward and displayed his most supplicating smile. Zia was the first to spot him.

"Señor Sherry, welcome. It's been a long time." Teresa, upon hearing of David's arrival, spun her legs from beneath the booth and faced him warmly, her cheek bearing the reddened flares of healing skin. She offered him a seat, patting the chair next to hers, but David ignored her, spewing a plethora of apologies her way.

"It's all right my love," said an understanding Teresa. "I'm sure you had a lot to do. Besides, Zia's been keeping me company. Catching me up on the latest gossip."

David diverted his eyes to the restaurant owner. "Thanks, Zia."

"*De nada, señor.* It's so seldom that I see her anymore."
She pushed herself away from the counter and showed
David to the table, helping him remove his coat before
being seated. "I'll be in the kitchen. Call me when you're
ready to order."

Teresa and David dined in near silence that evening,
anticipating the intense liaison they'd be experiencing
within the next couple of hours. Between them a solitary
candle flame wavered tenuously to the deepened sighs of
the two lovers. They ate and drank sparingly, their appetite
stemming more from their loins than their stomachs.

The walk home from Zia's was not a leisurely one.
The prospect of passion sent them scampering up the road
to David's house. Giggling like adolescents, they stormed
through the door and made their way to the bedroom,
where they sated themselves in unbridled lust.

The routine after-effects which generally left them
both spent and lifeless gave way this time to hunger.
Together they found their way into the kitchen. Teresa
removed some salami and cheese from the refrigerator,
while David searched for a package of stale crackers that
he'd stowed in one of the cupboards months ago. Putting
the combination together on a large plate, they took the
snack to the living room, placing it between them in the
middle of the couch. His cheeks stuffed with food, David
lit a small fire and sat back, watching it take hold. After a
moment, his eyes left the fire and he turned toward Teresa,
his expression somber.

"What is it?" she asked.

Unable to meet her stare, David peered again into the fire. "We...uh.... I think we need to talk." He paused for several seconds, formulating in his mind precisely what he needed to say. "It's about our future together."

Teresa felt her heart accelerate, but in her calmest voice queried, "And what about our future?"

David felt himself wavering and grabbed a handful of crackers, tossing them into his mouth. The pause was excruciating to Teresa, who tried prompting him with an animated shifting of her seat.

"Well," he began, "I've been thinking. I've never considered myself a quitter. Even as a kid I always tackled things head on. But there's one thing I chose to walk away from before coming here to Mancha Negra, and it's been bothering me a lot this year."

"Would it have something to do with your job back in the United States?"

"Why yes. How did you know?"

A pragmatic look crossed her face. "It's simple, really. Whenever you talk of your students back in San Diego, you seem so pained, so frustrated. I knew there was something wrong."

"You are amazing," said David with a shake of his head.

He reached for a piece of cheese, then placed it back on the plate. "You know, I love Mancha Negra. It's been a genuine breath of fresh air for me, and there's no question that I'd like to make this my permanent home someday. But first I need to go back and have another crack at those kids. And, I want you to come with me."

Upon hearing those words Teresa knew she could suppress her emotions no longer. Any fragments of dignity and aplomb she possessed up to that point were now fecklessly cast aside, and she shrieked in delight, snatching the snack dish from the couch and rushing next to him. "Oh, David, do you mean it? Do you really want me with you? Knowing that I'm a prosti—"

"Teresa, I don't care about that crap anymore. I want you as my wife. That is, if you'll have me."

"I can't believe I'm hearing this. David, I love you, I truly do." She put an arm around his shoulders and dropped her head to his chest, quietly digesting every syllable of the American's proposal. Teresa couldn't remember being happier than at that very moment. *A pity*, she thought, *that my family isn't alive to see this day.* Then Tito came to mind.

"But what of my uncle?" she said, searching his face. "He's getting older, and I'm all he has."

David calmly reminded Teresa of his conversation with her uncle, months earlier.

"There is no question he'd be delighted in our marriage," he said.

"But leaving him to go to the United States?" she persisted.

"Trust me. It's absolutely fine with him. San Diego is not that far away. He could fly up whenever he wished." This last piece of information seemed to greatly ease her mind. David felt her brush back against his chest. "Also,

I've been thinking that once we're in the States we can enroll you in a community college nursing program. With your command of English you'd have no problem. Can you imagine how proud Tito would be to know you're finally going to achieve your goal of becoming a nurse?"

Completely overwhelmed, Teresa could only shake her head in disbelief. She'd known many men in her young life, but none who could reach her as David had. Despite her giddiness, Teresa had the presence of mind to accept David's proposal, vowing never to make him regret his words.

Sometime during that night as they lay together, presumably asleep, Teresa withdrew from David's embrace and rose from the bed, where she dressed and left the house. Her lone figure moved effortlessly down the road, diminishing with each step through the late night mist. At the end of the earthen road she turned right and crossed through the abandoned plaza just beyond the village's gazebo. Stopping to remove a black scarf from her purse, Teresa placed it on her head and tied it tightly under her chin.

Off to her left beyond the gazebo she noticed the Club El Gato's singular cast of light, bouncing irregularly from the surrounding rooftops. Teresa cast aside the temptation to engage in melancholy, and pushed on until she reached the steps facing the façade of San Cristobal. Preparing to give thanks, she crept forward and humbly entered the sanctuary.

***

The following afternoon David left work precisely at 3:00, and headed quickly toward home. During the late morning he and his students had been interrupted by one of Tito's employees who blundered into the school, presenting David with a note. He apologized profusely for the disturbance, then backed out, closing the door gently behind him. Asking for his students' indulgence, David perused Tito's note, nodding his head as he went. The pimp was suggesting that they get together that day for a few hours of overdue conversation. He also indicated they do their palavering at a favorite fishing spot of Tito's, where he claimed the catfish just begged to be caught.

David barely had enough time to get home and pack himself something to eat and drink before he heard the roaring engine from Tito's recovered Imperial. The amused teacher ran to the door and held up three fingers. Perched grandly in the driver's seat, the pimp nodded and turned off the engine. David recalled how devastated Tito had been during the time his automobile was missing, moping about like a small child whose favorite toy had been taken away. Then came the recent news that it had been found by the police.

The fugitive Vega had abandoned it near a run-down hotel in Acapulco. When the news reached Tito, who was in the cantina's back room at the time, he became ecstatic. Tito threw open the doors and stepped into the bar, shouting, "They found her! They found her!" Witnessing the dumbfounded responses from his patrons, he explained, "My Chrysler. The police found my car!"

"Ah," came the aggregate sounds from those gathered at the tables and bar, and a hearty applause was presented to him.

With their fishing gear stowed in the large trunk, Tito and David headed into the back country for thirteen miles before turning onto a tar paved road that led to a fenced enclosure. Beyond the fencing the terrain changed dramatically, from the vivid, green vegetation of the jungle, to brown, rolling hillsides. Tito shoved the shift into park and pointed to a clump of trees rising from a small ravine about seventy-five yards away. David counted a couple of dozen cattle grazing lazily beyond the gate.

"We walk from here," the pimp announced.

"Tito, who owns this place? The scenery is breathtaking."

"It belonged to an old partner of mine who died a few years back. His wife runs it now. She's got a house farther up in the canyon."

Grabbing their gear, they opened the unlocked gate and hiked toward the ravine, where they came upon a crystalline creek that coursed down to a shallow pond bisected by a large, rotting tree. David followed his guide as they eased themselves down the embankment to the water's edge. The temperature dropped considerably under the shelter of the densely clumped trees. Both men hunched down, preparing their bait.

"How long have you been coming here?" David asked.

"Oh, many, many years. When my ex-partner bought this place we'd come here on Sundays and fish after early mass. I still enjoy it, although I don't get out here as much anymore. Even when the fish aren't biting it's a place to come and talk things out."

"And that's where Teresa comes in, huh?" David shot the pimp an empathetic wink.

"You've a very good head on your shoulders, my boy. Yes, that's partly the reason I chose this place. But mostly I brought you here because I enjoy your company." He cast his line into the creek near a patch of cattails. "I couldn't ask for a better man to marry my niece and give her the happiness she truly deserves. As you no doubt know, Teresa's a headstrong girl, but I'd always feared she might compromise her ambitions, what with the setbacks she's had to endure. By the way, you did know that Teresa paid off her parent's debts this past week?"

"No. She didn't tell me," said the stunned American.

Tito frowned and gave a banal shrug of his shoulders. "It's typical of Teresa, keeping her accomplishments to herself." No sooner had the pimp finished speaking when both men heard the clicking of Tito's reel, and watched the nose of the rod bend toward the stream. "You see, I've got one!"

Patiently the pimp played the line, then jerked mightily to his right, assuring his snag of a foot-long blue catfish. The stout white-bellied fish thrashed about the air, working its massive upper jaw against the hook in a futile attempt to free itself. Having just thrown in his own line, David pulled it aside, dropping it in a nearby thicket. He grabbed a net and stepped into the icy stream to scoop up the fish.

"Nice job, Tito. Guess I owe you a beer."

"It's my lucky hat, you know," he puffed, pointing to the Panama, pushed up high onto his forehead. "I've been wearing it for years, and it continues to bring me good fortune. Care to give it a try?"

David grinned, retrieving his own pole. "I just may before this day is out. First, let's see what the fishing gods have in store for me."

It wasn't until sundown that the two men shiftlessly hunkered down along the bank, having decided they'd had enough. Tito had caught six good sized catfish, while David totaled but one. However, his exuberance at catching the five-inch fry could not have been more animated had he reeled in a world record catch.

They returned to the car more weary than each cared to admit. The concoction of sun and beer had worked its magic on the men. Despite their condition, their mood was relaxed and cordial. Both men felt a deepening sense of friendship for one another.

Neither, however, felt compelled to address the painful subject of soon having to say farewell to the other, knowing they were fast approaching the finale of the school year.

It was twenty of nine when David reached home. He waved goodbye to Tito then turned toward the house. Recognizing the elongated figure of Teresa leaning against the door with her arms folded, David smiled openly.

"Did you have a good time?" she inquired, watching

him advance stiffly toward her.

"Great. Saw another of your uncle's talents. He caught a whole passel of fish."

"And you? How many did you catch?"

David reached her, poking a playful finger in her ribs. "A true fisherman never discusses his catch."

"It was that bad, huh?"

David's shoulders sagged, and with a saddened expression that would make a basset hound proud, extended a thumb and middle finger to a length approximating his solitary fish.

Teresa tossed her head back in laughter, duplicating David's measurement with her hand. "I guess, darling, it would sound more impressive if we measured it in millimeters." Tugging at his belt, she led him into the house. "Let's get you inside, Mr. Fisherman. I have a feeling you're famished."

***

Sitting alone in the kitchen, David gobbled down the last of the cashews from an open can. Not satisfied that it was completely empty, he turned the can upside down, tapping the bottom to retrieve the remnants of the nuts.

The teacher's spine ached from several hours of leaning over the breakfast table correcting test booklets. Unsure of the time, he guessed it was after midnight. Teresa had long since returned to the cantina after the two had had dinner.

He put down his red marking pencil and stood from the chair, massaging the small of his back. David peered mournfully at the table, acknowledging that he'd barely made a dent in his correcting efforts. "Shit," he said disparagingly. David walked to the kitchen counter and made himself a pot of strong coffee, grabbing his favorite mug from beneath the cupboard. Looking at the cup, he smiled, recalling the origin of the lightning-shaped crack that ran the length of the vessel.

The accident had occurred just after dinner. Teresa and David had been clearing the table when the young woman said nonchalantly, "Did Uncle Tito tell you I'm quitting?"

Her preoccupied lover, his hands filled with dishes, looked over at her. "Excuse me?"

"I said, did my uncle tell you I'm quitting the Club El Gato?"

A heavy soup spoon wedged between two plates dropped to the floor and, as David stooped to pick it up, he felt the dishes shift from his arms to his lap. Teresa rushed forward, catching several of the dishes before they fell. One casualty, however, was David's old coffee mug, a relic from his San Jose State days. It banged headlong into the spoon, causing a fissure from lip to base.

Refusing to let loose of the subject, Teresa queried, "You did want me to quit, didn't you?"

"You know the answer to that. It's something I've been hoping you'd say for months."

A pouting frown formed on her face. "Well, I thought you'd be a little more excited about it."

David put the dishes back on the kitchen table and

147

helped her with the ones she'd caught in her apron. He took both her hands and looked her squarely in the face. "I'm sorry if I don't sound excited, but I am, really. It's just that I've come to realize I would love you no matter what you did for a living. I'll always remember how sincere you were when you explained to me the purpose of your job. Quite honestly, honey, I didn't believe you then, but I do now. I think you do help people in a way, or at least that's your intention. Just look at the respect people here in Mancha Negra hold for you. What I won't miss, however, are men who have shared the same pleasures that you've given me. I want you all to myself."

Teresa protested. "But I've never given fully to any other —"

"And that's the way I want it to be. When your final day of work has ended, you'll be disrobing for only one man for the rest of your life, got it?"

Teresa beamed serenely. "Whatever you say, my darling. I'm all yours."

CHAPTER ELEVEN

The water heater was acting up again, forcing David to cut short his toilet. He opted to shave in the kitchen sink, but found Teresa had beaten him to it; she stood rinsing her hair under the faucet. Sneaking up behind her, David kissed her neck. "Save me some warm water, will you?" he asked.

"I'll try. Can you hand me that towel on the chair?" David fetched it and placed it around her shoulders. He waited until she'd finished, and then took the towel from her and begin to vigorously massage dry her hair.

"What's on your agenda today now that you have all this time on your hands?" David inquired.

"The first thing I have to do is to call the airport and confirm our reservations. Do you realize we're leaving here one week from Friday?" She withdrew from the sink and wrapped the towel around her head. "Ooh, David, I'm getting excited."

David grinned lewdly. "Good. That's the way I like to see you. Incidentally, remind me to call my mother this evening. I want to confirm our arrival time with her. You

149

know, she absolutely insists on our staying with her until we get settled."

Teresa pulled out a chair from the kitchen table and sat, wringing her hands nervously.

"I'm so afraid she won't like me."

"Are you kidding?" asked David, running a razor across his lathered face. "She'll love you. She told me the first thing she wants to do is take you shopping. Is there a better way for you two girls to initiate your ceremonial bonding?"

He finished shaving and ate only a portion of his breakfast, reminded by Teresa that he was running a little late for class. She helped him assemble some notes and handed him his daily planner, which he routinely checked each morning.

"Damn," he said, repeatedly jamming his finger at a specific page. "I'd totally forgotten. Señor Lopez and I set up a meeting for today at 4:30. I called him Monday to let him know we'd be moving back to the States at the end of the school year. Felt like hell laying it on him like that. Anyway, Lopez asked if he could drop by class this afternoon to discuss it further."

"You know, don't you, that he'll try everything in his power to persuade you to stay. Tito told me the school officials have been very impressed with you."

David closed the binder and placed it in his briefcase. "Let me tell you, it really wouldn't take much persuading on his part. What I'd like to do, however, is plead with him to keep me in mind for a teaching job sometime in the future." He looked at his watch and grimaced. "Yipes, gotta go. If you're keeping tabs, I owe you a kiss."

***

The first official heavy rains of the season began that afternoon and stopped abruptly before dawn the next morning, an intermission that lasted till the following afternoon. It came with a vengeance; seventy-two hours of non-stop precipitation. The fishermen, as usual, gauged these rains with indifference, and felt secure in sailing their skiffs far out to sea.

Villagers reacquainted themselves with the rapidly filling potholes that lined their walkways and streets. At higher elevations the roads winding down from the hills transformed into angry streams of mud, silt, and foliage, making motorized transportation impossible. But few complaints could be heard considering the past months of hot, dry weather they'd had to endure.

Standing on a chair with his back to the class, David attempted to adjust the hands on the wall clock. He calibrated the time with his wristwatch. "It looks as though you've got another ten minutes left. Those of you who are now done with your tests may leave. Just place them on top of your desks and I'll pick them up later. The rest of you, don't panic. You're still ahead of schedule. We'll take the first hour and forty-five minutes tomorrow to finish up the remaining section of the test."

Not surprisingly, all thirteen students had completed the first portion of their finals, and sluggishly rose to exit the school. As they gathered their materials, David reminded them that they all appeared to be doing well, and that they shouldn't dwell on tomorrow's final segment.

"Thursday you lucky young people will begin your holiday, while your poor, decrepit teacher will be slaving at his desk correcting your exams and compiling your grades for this term. You may stop by here Friday after 2:00 and pick up your report cards. Any questions?"

David scanned the room looking for hands, and having found none, declared the day over. Still not convinced that his students were sufficiently at ease, he stepped with them out into the rain, and yelled as they departed, "And for heaven's sake, relax. You've done this school proud."

The students, led by Carlos, branched out along the road in clusters, trudging slowly down the knoll, their feet heavily laden with packed-on sludge. For a quarter of a mile they continued silently, until they reached the main road past the church. As if on cue, each stopped and gravitated toward Carlos, who stood facing the schoolhouse. He wiped the rain from his face, then spoke up, his voice competing with the elements. "Sí, compadres, I know how you feel. We will all miss Profesor Sherry."

***

The granite stone skipped over the flat shallows of the estuary, bouncing twice before disappearing. "I used to be really good at this," David contended.

"You still are," said Teresa. She sat up from the sand, crossed her legs, and watched while David attempted to duplicate his earlier throw. After several more unsuccessful attempts he decided he'd had enough, aware that his arm was giving out.

"Whew, that's it. Better quit while I have some semblance of dignity left." He rolled down the sleeves of his shirt and dropped to his knees, kicking particles of sand onto their blanket. Teresa handed him a bottle of orange juice they'd been sharing.

"Finish it, darling — you look like you can use it."

David nodded appreciatively, gulping it down in three copious swallows. "Oh, that tastes mighty good." David rolled over on his back, placing his head in her lap. "Ah, Teresa, life is sweet. School's over, and the students all scored extremely high on their finals; Lopez has promised me he'll do all he can to get me reinstated to a similar teaching post, should we tire of San Diego; and last but not least, I'm returning home with the woman I love, ready to take on the world again."

Teresa looked down at him and smiled, bending forward to shield David's eyes from the sun. Using the hem of her skirt, she dabbed at a bead of perspiration forming on the bridge of his nose.

"I, too, am rejoicing, my sweet. I've completed the promises I made to myself, and now I can leave here without regret."

The faint sounds of church bells signaled the call to afternoon mass. Teresa eased David's head from her lap and stood, reaching for her sandals. She struck the heels of her shoes against each other, freeing them of sand, and then allowed David to slip them onto her feet. "Sure you won't join me for mass?" she asked.

"Not this time, honey. I've got to get back and finish packing boxes and washing some clothes."

"Okay," she said, "But do me a favor. Promise me you'll leave the housecleaning to me. I've seen your work, especially when it comes to finding places to store your magazines."

A crimson blush filled David's face. He reminded himself to check under the couch for a missing girlie magazine when he got home. Teresa hurriedly blew him a kiss and raced toward the church, churning up the sand with her long, graceful strides.

True to his word, David confined himself to packing and laundry, secretly amused at Teresa's keen eye and blunt diagnosis of his inept housekeeping. There was nothing he hated more than domestic chores. Taking a break for lunch, he grabbed a ham sandwich from the refrigerator and carried it with him to the utility room, where he dumped a basketful of clothes into the washer. The raucous chugging from the old Maytag muffled the sound of Teresa's entrance.

"Hello," she called, sticking her head into the room.

"Oh, hi," he muttered incoherently, a large chunk of sandwich wedged tightly between his teeth. "How wach churz?"

"Fine." Teresa turned her head and looked down the hallway. "I brought some company along. Why don't you come out and say hello?"

Looking puzzled, David pushed the remaining contents of the sandwich into his mouth. "Who ish it?"

Teresa said nothing but motioned for him to follow her to the kitchen.

"Hola, maestro," came a girl's voice.

"*Como está?*" another asked.

Upon entering the kitchen, David recognized the three girls from school. "Uh, hello girls, what are you doing here?"

None spoke, but in a gesture of giggles, deferred to Teresa. "The girls came to me after church and wanted to know when their esteemed teacher would be leaving. After I told them, they asked me if there was anything they could do to help us. So, here they are."

In mild protest David began to speak, but Teresa overruled him, explaining that this was typical small town hospitality. Reluctantly he acceded, watching helplessly as Teresa began distributing rags, cleansers, and a mop.

As the girls moved about the house, Teresa sided up to her lover. "Listen, gringo," she said soothingly, pushing him backwards toward the door. "If you want to make yourself useful, why don't you go down to the *pandería* and bring your students back some sweet rolls and cocoa? Señor Duran always opens his shop right after mass for a couple of hours."

The idea sounded appealing. David disregarded his umbrella and broke for the door, gambling that today's sky would continue its cloudless act, at least until he returned home. He judged the distance to be less than a mile, and knew a slow jog would get him there in a matter of minutes. But the winds remained constant and slapped hard at his loose-fitting shirt and pants as he left the house.

Within fifteen minutes, he reached the funnel of buildings running along the main street and eased into a leisurely canter. David stepped up onto the sidewalk and bypassed most of the shops until he came to the pandería. He entered, surprised to find Sergeant Arroyo and Tito standing at the counter. They appeared extremely engrossed in the day's selection of bakery items.

"Gentlemen," announced the American.

The two Mexicans turned toward David. Both were dressed rather casually, leading David to conclude they'd foregone the afternoon services themselves. Frankly, David felt relieved to be in the company of other sinners at that moment.

"Nice to see you, señor," said Arroyo.

Tito bulled his way from the counter and slapped a huge bear hug around David.

"Here to satisfy your sweet tooth?" the pimp inquired.

"Well, actually, I'm buying some pastries for three of my students who've offered to help me clean the house."

"Sure, sure," the pimp teased, wiping some sugared residue from his chin. "If you say so." He nudged David up to the counter. "Felipe," he called out. "Give the man anything he wants, and put it on my bill."

By now David knew protesting would be futile, and gave him a perfunctory, "Thanks."

"*De nada, Profesór.*" Tito pulled a large bill from his wallet and handed it to the proprietor. "Sorry I can't stay longer and chat, Señor David, but the sergeant and I have some legal matters to discuss."

The American snickered to himself, watching the pale looking sergeant fidgeting with his bag of sweets. David recalled that whenever he saw the two men together, poor Arroyo always seemed nearly apoplectic.

"Remember, Tito, you're coming to dinner tonight."

"My boy," said Tito, casting a Cheshire cat grin at David. "I've been thinking about it with great pleasure all day."

***

With the two saying goodbye, Arroyo patiently awaited his turn to offer his hasty felicitations over David's engagement to Teresa. Then, obedient as ever, the sergeant rushed to join the pimp at the door. They crossed the street and headed straight toward the plaza. When at last the sergeant felt he was a safe distance away from the pandaría and David, he spoke.

"Did you want me to tell him, jefe?" he asked.

Tito stopped in his tracks, and in a seething, quieted voice answered, "Of course not, you idiot. It shall be of no concern to them, especially now that they're leaving Mancha Negra in a couple of days." Nodding in agreement, the sergeant tightened his grip on the bag. "Anyway," Tito continued, "didn't you say the federal police are pretty sure they've got him boxed in?"

"Oh yes, that's true. I expect to hear of his arrest by sometime this evening. And don't worry, the press will not get wind of…of this morning's incident until your niece and Señor Sherry are well on their way back to the

States."

"Hmmph," snorted Tito.

They resumed their walk through the plaza, eventually seating themselves on a bench under a shaded palm. The men rested quietly, eating their sweet rolls while trying to erase the nightmare of Vega's recent escapade.

It was an hour ago that the sergeant had gotten the news and raced over to the cantina to inform Tito. He found the pimp at his usual table sipping a glass of milk.

"Excuse me, Señor Alvarez," he said, removing his cap. "May I speak to you...in private?"

Tito looked at him curiously for a moment. "In my office."

Within seconds after closing the door to Tito's office, Arroyo had explained all the sordid details. He described the federal police's recovery of a deserted car, which had been driven into a field approximately fifteen miles from Mancha Negra. The grisly remains of a young prostitute had been found in the backseat, smiling hideously at her discoverers. Everyone associated with the case knew positively that this was Vega's brutal trademark.

The pimp stirred from the swivel chair behind his desk and got to his feet, his jaw tense. "Goddamn you, Vega," he screamed, throwing the glass of milk against the wall.

CHAPTER TWELVE

"More peas?" offered Teresa, holding out a small, deep-dished bowl.

"No thank you, my dear." Tito put down his fork and drew the cloth napkin to his mouth, suppressing a burp. "I'm stuffed. This has been a wonderful dinner."

"I'm glad you enjoyed it," volunteered David. He reached for the wine and refilled Tito's glass. "I'd like to propose a toast, if you don't mind." Accordingly, Teresa and her uncle grabbed their glasses. "To the future Mrs. Sherry," said David.

"To the future Mrs. Sherry," echoed Tito. "And to your August wedding, which I'm really looking forward to attending. I hope I can persuade you to show me around your town after the festivities."

"I'd love to, Tito, but I'm afraid San Diego doesn't have quite the allure as does your Mancha Negra. It's just another overgrown, human ant colony. People moving about but really not living. Kind of pitiful when you think about it."

The pimp leaned back in his chair. "Well, it certainly

must have some redeeming qualities to have held a person of your distinction there all these years."

David laughed and stretched an arm around the back of Teresa's chair. "Boy, you're certainly right, honey. Your uncle is definitely a charmer. I don't know how he's remained single all these years."

"I think you're both very charming," said Teresa diplomatically. She got up from the table and removed some vanilla ice cream from the freezer. As she began scooping the dessert into three cups, a thunderous blow struck the outside of the door, followed by three additional raps.

Teresa ran to the door and threw it open. There stood Maximilian, his face taut.

"Perdone me, Teresa, but I must speak with your uncle." Not waiting for her to respond, Maximilian pirouetted by her and approached the two men.

"What is it?" bellowed Tito.

"It's the Club El Gato...it's burning!"

The stunned pimp took a step backwards and braced himself against the wall. However, the nearly full bottle of wine he'd consumed during the meal diverted much of his anxiety. "Let's go," he said to his henchman.

All four of them raced to the truck, with David and Teresa climbing into the flatbed. They sped down the hill, targeting the Chevy toward the hellish glow of the enflamed cantina. Maximilian broke hard, directing the pickup to within six feet of the entrance.

Tito was the first out, shouting orders to the small

crowd that was milling about the building. "Out of the way, please!" He leaped up onto the sidewalk in time to see his barman backing out of the swinging doors, his face blackened and awash with soot. Pepe dropped to his knees, hacking convulsively.

Lifting the man to his feet, Tito dragged him several yards from the cantina. "What happened, Pepe?"

The barman, wide-eyed and trembling, could do little other than stare helplessly at his employer. As his coughing subsided, he became more subdued.

"The fire...started coming through the back door.... Somebody blocked off the exit from the outside. I.... I tried to stop it, jefe, but the flames moved so quickly up the walls."

Pepe appeared to be close to losing consciousness, but Tito shook the man's shoulders, forcing him to remain alert. "Is there anyone still inside?"

"Don't know.... I think —"

Any further explanation was halted by a loud, crackling pop from a thick-set ceiling beam which had burned through its joint.

"Get away," yelled someone from the crowd. "It's going to cave in at any minute!"

Tito glanced up at his building, silently assessing the structure. "Pepe, do you think you'll be all right?"

The barman, despite his feeble appearance, nodded gamely. He looked consolingly at Tito's face, and at once realized the pimp's intentions. "Jefe, please, don't go in there."

161

Ignoring the man's pleas, Tito hastened to within a few feet of the smoky entrance. As he reached for a handkerchief with which to cover his mouth, a hand clutched his wrist.

"Wait," cried David. "Teresa said to tell you that help is on the way. Look down the street."

But the pimp wasn't listening. He freed himself from David's grip and surged forward.

"You're not going in there," threatened the American. Just as Tito reached for the swinging doors, David bolted into action, catching the Mexican by the waist and spinning him about. Tito's prized Panama hat flew from his head, ricocheting off a nearby post and landing in the street.

"Let me go, dammit. There may be people inside."

Tito grabbed David's right hand, bending back the joints of the ring and little finger. David howled in pain, instinctively pulling back his injured hand. Momentarily freed, Tito rushed into the cantina.

"No," David wailed. Shaking off the pain in his fingers, he stepped forward, preparing to enter, but a roar of flames fueled by a burst of oxygen from the opened doors drove him back.

"David, David!" Teresa's voice reverberated through the crowd of onlookers.

He spotted her at once, worming her way toward him. Sergeant Arroyo and Officer Muela were just ahead of her, leading a group of people carrying buckets of water. They aligned themselves in front of the Club El Gato and, in assembly line fashion, began dousing the cantina.

As quickly as buckets were emptied, another group ran forward to replenish them.

Stepping off the sidewalk, David converged with Teresa. From the harrowed expression in his eyes, the Mexicana surmised the fire was not the only problem. "David, what is it? The look on your face frightens me."

David didn't answer. He was distant, occupied in thought, his calculating eyes moving from her to the cantina and back again.

"Tell me, please. Is something else wrong? Is there something I should know?" she pressed. Before David could respond, Teresa gasped, suddenly realizing the situation.

"It's Tito, isn't it? Where's my — ?"

"Stay here," he commanded, the finality of his voice rising over the din of crackling timber and flame.

She placed her hands to her face and watched helplessly as David turned away from her and scrambled toward the cantina. He ran along the length of the building, weaving in and out of the brigades of bucketeers, searching for an entrance before turning the corner leading to the cul-de-sac of whorehouses. Behind the first house on the right he glimpsed a small break in a stone wall, which connected to a pathway leading to the cantina exit. David could see the charred remains of the door clinging tenuously to its hinges; the supporting posts and lintels, however, relatively undamaged. The danger, as the American saw it, came from the archway leading to the roof, which was already engulfed in flame.

163

David eased himself through the opening, instantly feeling microscopic ash penetrating his lungs. Despite the clouded mass of smoke in front of him, the actual blaze seemed to be contained to three or four pockets of the building's interior.

"Tito," David yelled, bumping into a corner table. He waited for a response, unsure of whether the old pimp could hear anything over the whooshing sounds of the inferno. With the heat and smoke sapping the moist lachrymal membranes of his pupils, David spat upon his hands, rubbing the substance into each eye. Blinking repeatedly, he worked his way through the labyrinth of overturned tables and chairs.

In his peripheral vision David caught sight of the bar, upon which laid smoldering embers of ceiling slats. Several smaller pieces resembling Fourth of July sparklers began to rain down on the bar's oily surface, caroming onto a throw rug in a fizzling display. The teacher willed himself forward, crushing them with the heel of his shoe. It was then that he discovered Tito's crumpled form sprawled beyond the bar.

David cautiously made his way over to the pimp, placing an ear on the man's chest. A singular eye opened. "David," he breathed. "You must leave me. Not safe, he —"

"Don't talk," countered the American. "Let's get you out of here."

David managed to get the pimp to a sitting position, then got behind him and pulled Tito to his feet. Once the

Mexican was able to steady himself, David placed an arm around the man's waist, pivoting him toward the rear door.

But within the short time David had spent in the burning building, the exit had become blocked. A concave section of wall crumbling silently against the door created a five-foot pyre of plaster and wood. Trying to bull his way through this would be suicide.

A frenzied scan of the room showed no other way out, and David's capacity to see even the most glaring objects began to worsen. He tightened his grip on Tito and brought his other arm over his eyes, hoping for even five seconds of clarity. And that's when he saw it: Tito's office, intact and untouched by the fire. Crossing the dance floor, he and Tito edged their way over to the room, and, to their surprise, found it slightly ajar.

David wedged a foot near the bottom of the door and swung it open.

The room was oppressively hot, with waves of low level smoke forming over their shoes. He turned slowly about the room, searching for an escape route. With the dead weight of Tito curtailing his movements, David guided the pimp to a chair, wedging Tito hard against the desk, his head tucked into his chest. Stepping away, David again surveyed the room.

Among the mementos and photos that graced Tito's darkly stained walls was a massive bookshelf that spread the length of the room. In the corner next to the bookshelf David saw what he thought were two columns of large, felt-covered books stacked from the floor to the ceiling. Their wavering caught his attention, and as he stepped closer, David realized he was looking at a narrow set of closed, full length drapes.

"That's it!" he exclaimed. "Our way out."

David rushed to the curtains, pulling apart the section closest to him. A hidden window approximating the same dimensions as the drapes seized his attention. Beyond the window David could see the vague outline of the abandoned hatchery across the road.

Returning to Tito, David found the old pimp disoriented and breathing irregularly.

"Just stay right here. I'll be right back." He offered the older man a quick reassuring smile. "I think our luck's about to change." David guided himself back to the curtains, grabbed the other section, and ripped them open.

There was no time to react to the human vise that clutched at his throat. The horrific recognition of the murderer Vega left David stunned, unable to comprehend what was happening. Stepping out from beneath the curtains, Vega drove the American back against the desk, hitting a corner of it with such force that it dislodged Tito from his chair. The pimp wavered for a few seconds, then dropped to the floor with a nauseating thud.

Vega bore even closer, forcing David's back to arch over the desk. The killer moved his head to within inches of the teacher, his nails sinking into the arterial channels of his adversary's throat. Unable to break the man's grip, David's head surged forward, smashing his skull against the bridge of Vega's nose.

"Ayee," screamed the shaken Vega. Bolting upright, he stepped back, releasing his grip from David's throat and cupping a hand over his bloodied, misshapen nose.

Remembering well the Mexican's ability to shake off injury, David continued the offensive, charging at Vega and throwing a shoulder into the murderer's midsection. The force carried both men through the window and out into the road, scattering shards of glass that rained over their prostrate bodies.

David lay stunned, unable to see his enemy, a resounding buzz emanating from his head. The taste of blood filtered through a corner of his mouth. Despite these distractions, he sensed a shadowy form cutting across his field of vision. David's eyes refused to focus, too exhausted to function, but his olfactory impulses picked up the acrid odor of Vega's breath on his face. In capitulation, David braced himself, anesthetizing whatever ending Vega had in store for him with thoughts of his beautiful Teresa. But the pain which was to follow had not yet arrived.

Reluctantly one eye cleared, conceding David a few precious seconds of vision. In front of him was the unmistakable sight of Vega. He kneeled no more than three feet from David, his mouth gaping, his good eye staring in disbelief. As if performing a muted mantra of death, Vega began to sway, rocking passively from side to side before toppling over at David's feet.

His mouth curled in contempt, David shifted his hips and extended his right leg, foisting the wretched corpse to the side of the road. As Vega lay face down, David stared incredulously at his blood soaked back, from which protruded an eight-inch dagger of serrated glass.

Directly behind the fallen body stood two shadowed Dantéesque figures outlined by the raging conflagration of the cantina. The larger of the two turned toward the flaming structure, while the other moved in David's direction. He tensed, digging his hands into the earth as he realized the approaching intruder seemed to be carrying a blunted, smaller version of what lay sticking out of Vega's back.

The languid locomotion of the oncoming form began to take shape. As it hovered over the bewildered American, David gasped, "Oh God."

Teresa, only now aware of the bloodied object she was holding, flung it aside and, using her blouse, wiped the crimson stains from her hand. "It's over," she stammered. She helped David to his feet in time to see Maximilian wading his way through the debris with Tito flung over his shoulders. Even at a distance it was obvious to the couple that Tito was in a bad way, despite the fact that he now appeared fully conscious. Attempting to mask his discomfort, the pimp demanded he be released from the giant. Gently, Tito was placed on his feet and, while holding tightly to Maximilian, stared disdainfully at the folded corpse. Gritting his teeth, he exclaimed, "I knew we'd get you."

As he heaved a defiant fist in the air, the explosion hit his chest. Tito's knees buckled and he lurched forward toward his niece. "Teresa!" His hands clutched tightly to his chest, the pimp dropped to his knees, caving onto the soft underbelly of the moist Mexican clay.

CHAPTER THIRTEEN

Dr. Ernesto Villa stifled a yawn as he left the ICU ward and moved along the blue tiled corridor to a small waiting room. At 3:50 a.m. the room was virtually silent, its only two occupants seated together on a large, faux-leather chair.

David's head rested against the wall. He was unaware of Teresa's soft purring breaths as she lay cradled in his arms, her legs in a fetal position. Outside the hospital, negotiating the opening of a new pack of cigarettes, paced an apprehensive Sergeant Arroyo.

The instant Villa entered, David bucked forward, waking Teresa in the process.

"Please don't get up," said the doctor. Teresa slid from David's lap to the unused portion of the chair.

"Tell me, Doctor, how is he?" queried David.

"He's resting right now," replied Villa, "but breathing on a respirator." The doctor glanced at the chart in his right hand. "I must commend the fast actions of Sergeant Arroyo. It took great skill to get Mr. Alvarez here as quickly as he did. Had you taken him to the clinic instead of here to Acapulco, he might not have made it. They don't have the facilities to handle such serious disorders."

Dr. Villa pulled up a chair beside Teresa and David and sat on its edge. "As you're probably aware, señorita, your uncle shows symptoms of a massive heart attack stemming from the right side of the aorta. Additionally, tests have revealed that his liver is engorged, a moderate hepatic dysfunction that commonly occurs in this situation."

"What can be done for him?" Teresa asked, composing herself as best she could.

"For now, he'll certainly need lots of rest, oxygenation, and an immense diet change. But the most urgent matter is to find the cause of his heart failure."

David and Teresa looked at one another, then rose together, preparing to thank the doctor for his efforts. But Dr. Villa continued to sit, uncomfortably formulating his concluding words. He sighed heavily while inadvertently toying with his wedding ring. Finally he spoke, his voice calm and even.

"May I be frank with you both? I've never been able to sugar-coat situations like this very well. I think it's more important for those concerned to know exactly what's going on." The doctor shifted his eyes from one person to the other, and sensing no objections, he continued. "Señor Alvarez may very well survive this and live several more years in the process. However, the damage to his organs, as I see it, is extremely debilitating. I doubt very much whether he'll be actively mobile again. The statistics are just not in his favor, I'm afraid."

Teresa drew back into the chair, a noticeable tremor moving from her arms to her shoulders. "Are you saying, Doctor, that he may be bedridden the rest of his life?"

"What I'm saying is his life as you knew it only hours ago will no longer be the same. He'll need lots of care, not just physically, but psychologically. Do you feel you have the capacity to handle that? I want you to consider this very carefully. If you don't think you can do this, we do have excellent nursing facilities here in Acapulco. They're designed to relieve you of that burden; in essence, to provide you with an alternative."

"I just.... I...." Teresa, burdened by this sudden decision, looked pleadingly at David for counsel. She'd grown to rely on the American more than she cared to admit. Teresa grabbed his hand in an attempt to pull him nearer to her.

But David held his ground, his demeanor surprisingly decisive. He looked steadily at the tired face across from him. "There is a second option, Doctor."

CHAPTER FOURTEEN

For the two vacationing Toledo chiropractors, Acapulco was becoming a bit of a bore. Michael Fain and Len Seacourt tried their best to shun the hustling condo sales representatives working each street corner, and spent countless hours maneuvering in and out of curio shops in the hopes of bringing back souvenirs that were actually made in Mexico.

To make matters worse, the intense rains of late September had scattered the contingent of bikinied beauties from the beaches. With only two days remaining of their seven day, six night vacation package, Michael and Len decided to become adventurous.

They tossed their bottled waters and cameras into their rented convertible and headed south, hoping to capture the magic of authentic Mexico somewhere down the road.

Without a planned destination, Mike and Len traversed a maze of narrow roads until they found themselves on the outskirts of Mancha Negra. Len stopped short of entering the village, pulling to the side of the road.

"Now will you look at this? Definitely what I'd call

173

the real thing."

Mike dropped a map into his lap and peered through the insect-dotted windshield. "What are we waiting for? Let's check it out."

As the car idled its way through town, both men gawked at the local architecture and the colorfully faded shops which led toward the beach.

"Looks like a pretty old town," commented Len.

"Yeah, the buildings look really run down...except for that one."

Mike pointed to an outlandishly colored cantina at the end of the street. Pink stucco walls supported a tiled roof, upon which was centered a small neon sign whose vertical letters read, *Club El Gato.*

"I don't know about you, Len, but I'm pretty thirsty. Care for a cerveza or two?"

"Absolutely. Lead on, partner."

Mike parked the car and the two crossed the street, entering the cantina in tandem. They pushed their way through the swinging doors and bypassed the bar, where a handful of elderly men had gathered, telling fishing tales to one another for the thousandth time.

"Hey, take a look at that," signaled Len, tapping his friend on the shoulder as they were about to take a table. "Three tables over. Two fine looking ladies. I think they're staring at us."

Mike rotated his chair to get a better angle. "I think you're right. Listen, I'm going to get us those beers. Hold the fort, 'cause this could be our lucky day." Hoping to catch the attention of the women, Mike strutted to the bar. "Two beers, *por favor.*"

The wiry little barman nodded, bringing up the chilled bottles from a trough under the counter.

"Thanks," said the chiropractor, slapping a heavy, metallic peso on the counter.

"Is there anything else?" asked Pepe.

Surprised at the barman's English, Mike stiffened. "Well, uh, as a matter of fact there is. Can you tell me anything about those two girls over there?" He shifted his head subtly toward their table.

A casual grin spread across Pepe's face. "Oh, señor, they are local girls. Very pretty, no?"

"Yes indeed. Do you know if they're with anyone? I mean…are they married or something?"

Pepe chuckled and breathed into a shot glass, wiping it dry. "I think not, but if you'd like to meet them I know someone who can introduce you." He turned his back on the two men for a moment, placing the glasses below the counter.

Len felt his heart skip. "Really? Who?"

"That man in the corner reading the newspaper. If you wait one minute, I'll get him."

With an exuberant step, Len dashed back to where Mike was seated, slamming the frothy beers onto the table. He leaned into his friend, his words clipped and whispered.

"We're in luck, pal. The bartender said that guy over there in the suit knows those girls, and he's going to introduce us to them."

Mike beamed broadly and looked with anticipation at the figure hunched behind the jukebox. Both men watched as the man folded his paper upon hearing Pepe approach.

The barman brought with him a demitasse of coffee, balanced skillfully in one hand. As he bent over the table, Pepe mouthed a few words to the man in the suit, whose eyes shifted toward the two Americans.

Pepe returned to his bartending duties while his well-dressed patron took a quick sip of coffee, then got up and approached Len and Mike.

"Hello," he said nervously, with a slight nod of his head. "I understand you gentlemen are interested in those two ladies over there." The man turned and waved a hand in their direction, beckoning them forward. Rising seductively, the two young whores sashayed forward. "This dark haired lady on my left is called Zonia, and the little one here with the big eyes is Felicia. And my name is Sherry…David Sherry."

David paused for a moment, and glanced across the room at a dimly lit table near the entrance. He shrugged his shoulders and held his palms outward, as if wondering whether he'd done everything correctly.

A pair of approving grins from an elderly man in a wheelchair and a dark haired Mexicana greeted him. David acknowledged them with a nervous smile and turned back to face the two Americans. "And now, gentlemen, I guess we have a little negotiating to do."

ABOUT THE AUTHOR

J. D. Chaney is a retired teacher and short story writer who lives in the San Francisco Bay Area. He has published dozens of fiction and non- fiction stories throughout England and the U.S. When not writing he enjoys running, watching Bay Area sports, reading and traveling the world with his family.

Made in the USA
San Bernardino,
CA